Caroline – who can do the splits and who could have been a world-famous ballerina

Caroline Plaisted,

the author of *Cringe!* and *Do I Look Like I Care*, was told by her teachers that only clever people could work in publishing and magazines. Despite that, she worked in publishing for fourteen years before starting to write her own books. She has had nearly forty books published, for children and adults, and is also the editor of various educational magazines. Caroline lives in Kent with her two children, two cats and two dogs.

Cherry – who makes necklaces out of her old earrings and who definitely can't do the

Cherry Whytock,

the illustrator of *Cringe!* and *Do I Look Like I Care?*, has recently become a 'townie'. This has made buying face cream and collecting shoes much easier. She lives with a big fluffy cat, a boxer dog called Lily (who is in love with a dachshund) and her husband. Her gorgeous grown-up daughters are both about to become fabulously famous and they come and visit henever they need to borrow ake-up or shoes!

Also by Caroline Plaisted and Cherry Whytock

Cringe!

Do I Look Like I Care?

Caroline Plaisted
& Cherry Whytock

MACMILLAN CHILDREN'S BOOKS

First published 2005 by Macmillan Children's Books
a division of Macmillan Publishers Limited
20 New Wharf Road, London N1 9RR
Basingstoke and Oxford
www.panmacmillan.com

Associated companies throughout the world

ISBN 0 330 43658 9

3 5 7 9 8 6 4 2

A CIP catalogue record for this book is available from
the British Library.

Typeset by Nigel Hazle
Printed and bound in Great Britain by Mackays of Chatham plc, Kent

For Hannah – who has done a lot of CRINGE-ing!

Hannah - who is fab!

CONTENTS

CATCHING UP/
IT'S A BOY THING

Do parents ever give up trying to embarrass you? Not! Just when I thought I'd got them the way they should be, after the painting thing, they've gone and blown it.

My dad was the reason for the painting thing. All my life my dad's been just so not cool. He runs this seriously sad shop. It's called FLOWERDEW AND SONS AND DAUGHTER. (I'm the lucky daughter. Like he thinks I'm ever going to be seen dead working there?) He says it's a health food emporium. It sells lots of brown food — food that's brown even before it's cooked. My dad's name is Marcus, and he thinks we should call him Marcus instead of Dad. Per-lease!

Anyway, Dad spends all his spare time painting these gigantic pictures. Mostly of naked people. How gross can you

1

Some of Dad's Hawaiian shirts have short sleeves — he likes to feel the breeze around his arms—UGH

Don't know why Nono never seems to knit enough tank top to cover Dad

Frank's version of 'Stars and Stripes' has some pretty fruity words in it.

Probably going to poo on Dad's shoulder

You would think that now he's a 'FAMOUS' artist he could dress a bit trendier

looking miserable as usual

big stinky fart area

Wearing his Yuk sandals again, never, ever, ever, wears socks

get? Our house used to be full of them but then he was 'discovered', according to my mum. Actually what that meant was that he had a painting chosen for some exhibition in London. Then suddenly everyone seemed to think he was a brilliant artist, and he sold all these pictures and went to

Ben, listening to some grotty grungy stuff

he says he's growing his hair!

Dad in his 'look at me, I'm an artist' outfit

Sucky uppy, uppy chucky, double yukky Hugo Poogo

paint brushes

Mum in her new American trousers with her new American hairdo which has gone a bit weird

ME Amaryllis, would-be superstar and totally cool chick — if it wasn't for this pukey plastic rain cape and my freaky family

Les leaving

These are my BROTHERS — pity me...

America and sold some more. That was when things began to look up. Incredibly my dad got paid for the paintings. Real money. Money that buys Miss Sixty jeans and Skechers. Like my dad was going to buy things like that — NOT! He bought an old World War II motorbike with a sidecar (this is not a joke) and a couple of flowery shirts for himself. And for me? A pair of Manilos and an American baseball jacket to wear on the bike. Like, yeah, right! Me? I got a totally disgusting raincoat with this hat that was an umbrella! Worse! It had windscreen wipers that hung down from the brolly bit! Still, I suppose my dad did seem to chill out a bit. Except of course for the beret he started wearing. I mean, HOW SAD IS THAT?

hope the light bulb won't glow through the compost

Got to make sure Poojo the Pathetic doesn't sneak on me

COMPOST

My mum (she's called Mary but wishes I'd still call her
Mummy — that's Mum with an M Y on the end — N O spells
NO!) went to America with my dad. When she came back —
well, it was freaky! She'd got this trendy spiky hair and was
even wearing a bit of make-up! And she'd got some vaguely
cool clothes. She even bought some for me —a pair of Armani
jeans. Only they weren't really Armani because they said
Armini on the label. That's with two 'i's. But then I suppose if
you are as old as my mum (she's already thirty-eight) you just
don't understand. My Mum is a counsellor. She sees the

4

mum being poetic—
bet she's trying
to think of something
to rhyme with
'scummy water'—
could be 'gorgeous
daughter' i.e. ME

weirdos that she counsels in Ben's old bedroom. (Ben's my older brother, but I'll tell you about him in a minute.) But what my mum would really like to be is a Poet. She belongs to this Circle of Poets. Basically they are a bunch of nutcases. They get together once a week to read each other the desperate poems they've been writing. Yawn, yawn.

Now comes the awful truth (yes, it gets worse). I have TWO BROTHERS. I mentioned Ben before. His real name is Geoffrey. Sad or what? Natch, he changed his name to Ben.

clothes peg—
put on nose
before approaching

HEALTH WARNING

Ben's
socks

Jake

Ben used to say that he was a Street Poet but these days he talks about himself as a Performance Artist. What this means is that during the day, Ben spends all his time in his bedroom. This is in the cellar of our house, and it has no windows. Ben sneaks in and out of the house from the cover over the old coal-hole. Most of the time, I don't see much of Ben. But – big BUT. Ben has this band. They're called GOB, and they've managed to blag their way into some pop star competition called MUSIK MANIAKS. They are singing a song called 'I don't want to get out of bed'. Enough said really. My ex-boyfriend Jake plays guitar. (He used to really fancy me, but I told him where to get off when he puked on my shoes at my Auntie Melissa's wedding – but that's another story [called Cringe! – go out and buy it now!].) For some strange reason which I can no longer work out, I used to think that Jake was dead cool and sophis. When he did the rainbow cake thing on my shoes, I realized that he was totally NOT dead cool and sophis and not even very interesting. So I went off him in a BIG way.

I've no idea what the other guitarist is called because he never speaks. Actually he's only awake when the band are playing – the rest of the time he's in a coma. Then I have a younger brother. He is called Hugo (Poooo-go!). He is:

- smelly
- slimy
- a PAIN
- Hugo is the creep to out-creep all creeps.

Since his appearance on the local telly programme when Dad went to America, Hugo has gone even weirder than he was before. He is always smiling at his own reflection in things. And he has decided that he wants to be a wildlife presenter on telly. Hugo is always taking our dog Giggles out for nature hunts (I don't know why Giggles is called that because he is a really bad-tempered dog. And he really honks — talk about Kennel Number Five — phewee!).

Poogo being pathetic

has to look at himself in anything shiny

Keeps a squashed frog in his pocket — he scraped it off the road — UGH

My BOYFRIEND
Tarquin

I think it would be a really good idea if Hugo went off on a wildlife expedition and got completely lost in the jungle. Oh dear, how sad that would be — hee, hee!

You know I said that Jake was my ex-boyfriend until the puking on the shoes incident? Well the only good thing about that was that Jake's brother is called Tarquin. And Tarquin is fit.

AND TARQUIN IS MY BOYFRIEND! AMARYLLIS ROSANNA LILLIAN FLOWERDEW HAS A BOYFRIEND! He started to be my boyfriend on my thirteenth birthday. Tarquin is tall and cool. He's got this cute face and wears ace clothes. Everyone at school is like – 'Hey, Amaryllis and Tarquin are going out!' You bet we are!

One of my other best things is Xanthe. She is my best friend, and she is really beautiful. We have been friends for ever. Things have been sad for Xanthe. Her mum (who is also gorgeous) and dad (a bit of a Westlife/George Clooney/Darius/Sting lookalike) have just split up. Xanthe has been

dead sad about it. But the good news is that Xanthe and her mum are just about to move into a house down the road. How brill is that? Brill rating = Infinity out of 100!

My final best thing is Nono. Nono is my granny, and she is just fab. She's not one of those grannies that smells of sour milk and wee. And she's not one of those exhausting

grannies who wears a track suit all the time and goes off climbing mountains and running marathons. But she is completely cool:

☆ Nono is into gadgets.
☆ She's got one of those flat screen tellies, and when you watch it it's like being in the cinema.

Me, styled by Xanthe

✩ And now she's got one of those mobile phones that takes movies.

✩ She even drives a sports car.

✩ Nono is the sort of person who smells like cakes and flowers.

✩ I love Nono.

✩ Even her dog is cool. He's called Brian and he never does anything wrong. (Giggles hates him.)

✩ Nono is a brilliant knitter — she can knit anything.

At the moment she is knitting loads of things with Mrs Baxter. Mrs Baxter lives next door to us with too many dogs to count. She breeds dogs and calls them Baxter Terriers. The only problem is that every dog looks completely different so her breed can't be registered. Anyway, the reason that Nono and Mrs B are doing so much knitting is because of Napoleon. No,

hairy ears - UGH!

Nono knitted Nappie's Napoleon hat

Nono knitted this too in Doug's favourite football team's colours

Doug and Mel and Nappie

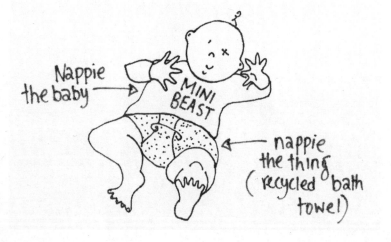

not the French bloke. Napoleon is my cousin — ANOTHER BOY!

So, Napoleon. He's just been born and is the son of my dad's sister Melissa and her boring anorak of a husband called Doug. Melissa, Doug and Napoleon live on a canal barge called 'Doug 'n' Mel' — so sad but true.

For some reason I can't understand, everyone seems to think that I should think Napoleon is great and that I will want to play with him all the time.

Question: What planet is my family on?
Answer: Planet SAD!

 TEXT to Xanthe: WOTCHA!

SO IS THIS IT?

Like I said, Xanthe is just the best, best mate a girl could have. I was completely freaked when Tarquin (THAT'S MY BOYFRIEND!) asked me out. It was my thirteenth birthday, and Tarqs texted me on my new mobie (Nono gave it to me for my birthday so Mum and Dad — who had said I couldn't have my own mobile under any circumstances — couldn't take it away from me — NONO FOREVER!). His message said CN I C U? Like you can't guess what I texted back?

Xanthe helped me get ready. I wore:

☆ *my cut-off jeans*
☆ *my Divine T-shirt*
☆ *my sparkly bangles (given to me by Xanthe)*
☆ *my tummy lace (lent to me by Xanthe)*
☆ *my flip-flops — customized by moi.*

16

We're talking Hawaiian Beach Babe!

Xanthe did:

☆ *my make-up*
☆ *my hair*
☆ *my nails.*

Yum, yum, kiss, kiss!

Can't move my head much in case my hair goes flat

We customized this with frilly bits and beads and felt-tip pens

this our Hawaiian Beach Babe look

Divine

she did lend it to me!

I have essential supplies of lip gloss and hair goo and my phone so I can text Xanthe

Xanthe's mum had some fringing left over from her curtains

Stuck sequins on my flip-flops

I'd never been on a date before. (OK, this is the truth bit: so I said before that Jake was my Ex, but actually he was never really my boyfriend. I just fancied him, and I am sure he fancied me, but he just never mentioned it. When he did the puking thing I sacked him from my life FOREVER.) I'd read loads about dates in magazines so I knew that the boy turns up on your doorstep with a bunch of roses for you and looks longingly in your eyes all night, while he tells you you are gorgeous, and he's going to love you forever because You Are The One.

19

NOT!

This is what happened:

*1 Tarquin turned
up at our house.*

2 He did not take me in a chauffeur-driven car.
3 We walked to McDonald's, and it was raining!

4 Turned up at McDonald's cunningly disguised as a soggy Hawaiian Beach Babe.

5 Was eating my McFlurry when boys from school turned up.

6 Tarqs and the boys spent the rest of the evening talking about the footie match.

7 Tarqs took me home.
8 HE KISSED ME!

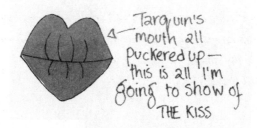

Am not sure what a kiss is meant to be like in real life. Now I think about it I suppose it is impossible for spit not to be involved. Kiss, kiss without the yum, yum really. Rang Xanthe from my mobie when I got home and was in bed.

She said, 'So what was it like?'

And I told her.

'So no flowers then?' she asked.

'No,' I said. 'But he did buy me a Happy Meal so I did get the fluffy toy.'

'Bless!' Xanthe said.

Which was true. Only I was still hungry — after all, it was only a Happy Meal.

'Did you S-N-O-G?' Xanthe whispered.

Was honest and said we'd just kissed. But I didn't mention the bit about the spit. Still, at least Tarqs wasn't wearing a brace. DISGUSTING OR WHAT? There's a girl at school who's always going on about the boys she snogs and she wears a brace. One of those ones that looks like train tracks. No one believes that she really does it. I mean what about all that food that must get stuck in the metalwork. GROSS!

But who cares about other people's spinach when True Love is happening in my life? Told Xanthe that when we'd got to my house, Tarqs said, 'Can I see you next week then?' and I said, 'OK.'

The second date will be much better than the first date, I'm sure.

HE CANNOT BE SERIOUS!

My father is PATHETIC!

Was in my bedroom on Sunday afternoon when he called all of us into the kitchen for something he called a Family Conference. Think this is one of the things he must have read about while he was in America. Something he thinks is trendy. NOT!

Mum had made tea. Mum's teas are nothing like the ones Nono does.

Nono's teas have:

☆ *delicious yummy home-made cakes*
☆ *lots of Coke*
☆ *wagon Wheels*
☆ *nothing brown except chocolate*

Mum's teas have:

     👤 *one home-made cake that has burnt bits on and weighs a ton*

     👤 *her version of lemonade which is home-made and has things floating in it*

     👤 *bread which Dad has made and it has gritty bits in it.*

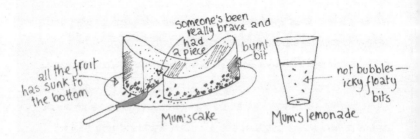

someone's been really brave and had a piece

burnt bit

all the fruit has sunk to the bottom

Mum's cake

not bubbles — icky floaty bits

Mum's lemonade

Was dead cross with Mum and Dad when they told us about the FC. I'd been planning to go and watch a new DVD at Nono's. It was just so not fair!

     Hugo was first in the kitchen doing his 'Oh, darling Mummy, can I help you?' cheesiness. Dad had let Frank out of his cage. I don't think I mentioned Frank earlier, did I? Frank's my dad's parrot. He was given to Dad by some old man who used to live in our street. The old man had been a sailor. Frank is much more cool than Giggles. Like Giggles is OK, but he's just boring. Frank, though, is never boring. Frank swears all the time. Nono said once that she thought the old man had taught Frank to say rude words. Dad

Dad says that this is Frank being friendly — wonder what he'd do if he was being unfriendly??

doesn't seem that bothered — except he does get all stressy when Frank swears at his customers in the shop.

At the Family Conference, Frank was sitting on Dad's shoulder, pulling at Dad's hair. Ben was last to turn up. He came out of the cupboard under the stairs. That's the way out of his cellar inside the house. He didn't say anything — as usual. He just kind of grunted and slumped down.

My Mum did her 'Darling Geoffrey' bit and ruffled his hair. Ben just ducked out of her way and cut a slice of Dad's bread. Big mistake. You can't slice Dad's bread. It just disintegrates into crumbs. Ben didn't seem to care though. He just kind of shovelled the crumbs into his gob — as opposed to his GOB, ha ha!

Why would anyone want to touch this?

Wonder if her earlobes will stretch and get as dangly as her earrings?

looks OK until you try and eat it

When we were all sitting down, Dad told us his news. Am so angry I couldn't even ring Xanthe to tell her. DAD HAS REALLY LOST IT THIS TIME. He told us that he had been thinking about the Fortunate Position the money he'd got for his paintings had put us in. And I'm thinking too right — like we can buy proper food for a change. And a telly. And a car (instead of going everywhere in Dad's pieces-stuck-together shop van). And we can send Hugo away on some nature trip For A Very Long Time. And loads of clothes and shoes for me — natch.

But does Dad say that that's what we are going to do? No. What Dad says is that he and Mum have been Thinking. This is always dangerous. Mum and Dad have apparently been Thinking how unfair it is that they have been given so much dosh when we don't really need it.

Are they mad? Unfair? Unfair to who? Of course we need it!

Then it got EVEN WORSE!

Mum and Dad said that they had Made A Decision. The decision is that they are going to share the money round. Only not with me, Hugo and Ben. No, my mum and dad are going to give all the sponduliks to a Good Cause. And apparently a gooder cause than their own children is everyone in The Community.

Second-hand Bank plc

12.56 10
60031 7891011

Pay: The Community Centre

£ 2 and some noughts

Toadsadosh

M.Flowerdew

mmm 10756314 9064

22216h! this could have paid for really good hair extensions, wads of cloth piles of make-up, a trip to Florida and so much mo

MY MUM AND DAD ARE GIVING THE PAINTING
MONEY TO THE COMMUNITY CENTRE SO THAT IT CAN
BE MADE POSH.

The Local Sensation

OUR OWN MARCUS FLOWERDEW TO CREATE COMMUNITY PORTRAIT

THE CENTRE

GOB

BABE

MARCUS AND MARY FLOWERDEW WITH THEIR DELIGHTFUL CHILDREN BEN, HUGO AND AMARYLLIS

I bet there'll be a bit in the local paper and it will look like this— AAARGH!

What is wrong with our house being posh for once?
Then my mum said that the council had been so
pleased with being given all Dad's money (like surprise!) they
had asked Dad to paint the outside of the Community Hall.
With a mural. And the mural is going to have all of us on it.
I THINK I AM GOING TO DIE!

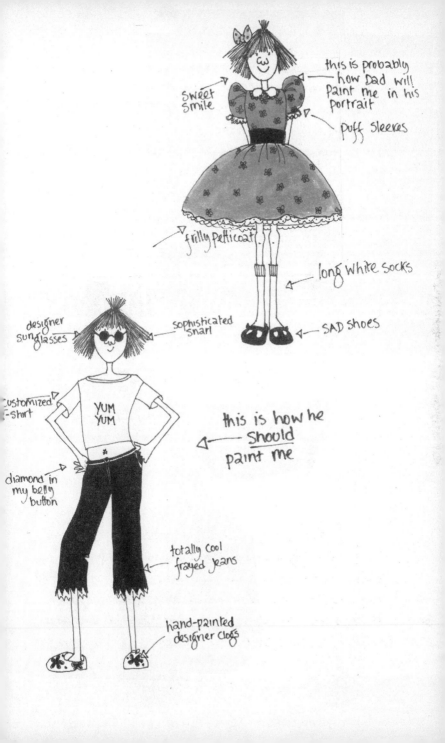

Mum said it like I was supposed to be pleased. Hugo Poogo is so sucky uppy that he said he thought it was a brilliant idea and immediately went into one of his poses like he was practising for the mural. Ben just grunted a bit louder than normal and disappeared down into the cellar. I just said 'How could you?' and went down the road to see Xanthe.

Xanthe and her mum only moved in a few days before. So they were still unpacking stuff. Tasmin is Xanthe's mum, and she has got this mega-long hair. I'm growing mine so that it's going to look like hers soon. Tasmin is really clever, and when she was still with Xanthe's dad, they had this really gorgeous house. It was dead stylish with lots of exotic arty

Xanthe's new house – love the heart-shaped number!

next door's cat

Nono's homemade fudge

xanthe's mum has already put up these gorgeous sparkly curtains

stuff. Tasmin is a jewellery designer, and she used to import jewellery from India and sell it to shops here. But she kind of slobbed out when she was splitting up with Xanthe's dad. She went a bit Mrs Track Suit — and we're not talking Juicy here. She stopped working and just stayed on the sofa. Mrs Sofa Track Suit.

But now they've moved house, Xanthe's mum's going back to her old self. I mean my mum could never look that smart if she was sorting out the house. When I got there on the Sunday, Xanthe and Tasmin had started to sort out Xanthe's room and the living room. The living room was looking pretty together. In one corner Tasmin explained that she'd got her work space. In their old house she had a whole room upstairs that was her studio. In this house they don't have as much space.

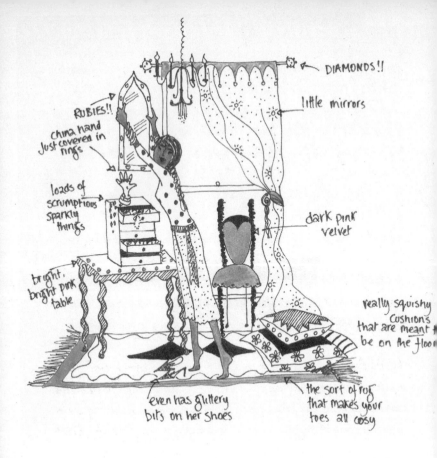

DIAMONDS!!

little mirrors

RUBIES!!

china hand just covered in rings

loads of scrumptious sparkly things

dark pink velvet

bright, bright pink table

really squishy cushions that are meant to be on the floor

even has glittery bits on her shoes

the sort of rug that makes your toes all cosy

But in the corner of the living room there was all this gorgeousness. Lots of sparkling things — mirrors, necklaces — even pens. My mum's office in our house is pants! Tasmin's office area is scrummy.

Tasmin even made us a scrummy meal too! We sat on the floor and ate it like in an exotic musical. It was cool.

Back home though it is just so not cool. It is a disaster!

 TEXT to Tarqs: THNKG OF U! T X

34

THE WONDER OF
WOOLIES

Went to Nono's after school again because I am totally fed up with going home and finding GOB slobbing around and rehearsing all the time. Worse, GOB have been acting even more weird than usual. Since they got through to the final of that MUSIK MANIAKS telly series they seem to care about their hair a lot. Ben has even started to use gel! He used to just rely on the natural grease before. Mum used to complain because he didn't wash his hair before. He said it was because he was allowing the natural oils to settle. Like per-lease! Every time it rained his head used to steam, and it smelt even worse than Giggles does when he gets wet. Yuck!

Anyway, with GOB thinking they actually have talent and behaving like pop idols, and Mum's saddos being

counselled in the house, and Hugo doing his posing and looking at himself in the kettle, I keep away. Plus Nono always has something scrummy to eat. On this afternoon, she'd made:

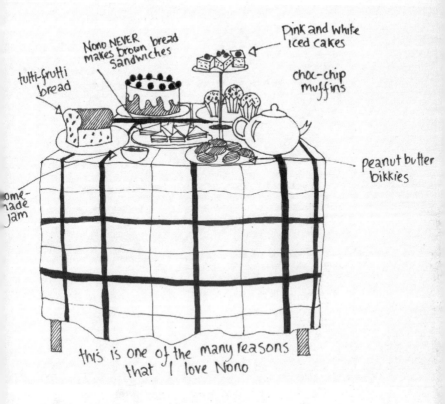

tutti-frutti bread

Nono NEVER makes brown bread
Sandwiches

Pink and white iced cakes

choc-chip muffins

home-made jam

peanut butter bikkies

this is one of the many reasons
that I love Nono

- ☆ double choccie-chip muffins
- ☆ her own sausage rolls
- ☆ little pizzas
- ☆ jam tarts
- ☆ white bread sandwiches
- ☆ peanut butter cookies
- ☆ pink and white iced cakes
- ☆ tutti-frutti bread.

bet she wouldn't want Giggles to lick her face

I think this might be her nightdress

DOGGY BAG

Mrs Baxter

never, ever, ever takes her boots off

Mrs Baxter was at Nono's when I got there. She's really cool and does things like pass me bottles of lemonade and Coke across the garden fence. When Nono came to stay with us (that was when Mum and Dad were doing their celeb bit round America before their brains turned to jelly, and they gave it all up) she got on really well with Mrs Baxter. Now

Baxter baby back pack

Mrs Baxter's back

often keeps her knitting needles here

Mrs Baxter's dogs had to go and sit in the other room because they kept chewing the balls of wool

wonder if her feet go mouldy inside her boots?

they hang out together doing granny sort of things. Like their knitting and baking and watching Countdown on telly.

In fact when I got to Nono's, Nono and Mrs B were sitting in the living room surrounded by loads of balls of knitting wool. They were clicking away together and listening to some brass band music. It was like a granny knitting fest. They'd been making things for Napoleon. There were:

☆ a billion pairs of little booties
☆ about ten hats like the ones burglars wear that only have slits for eyes

39

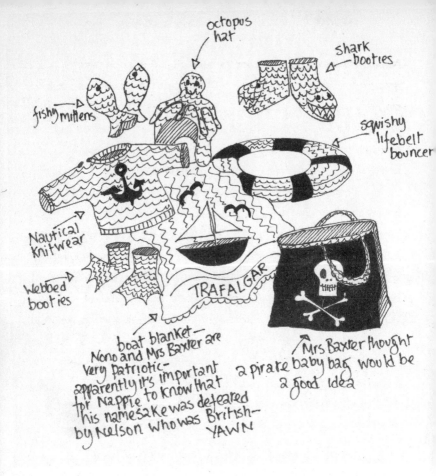

octopus hat

shark booties

fishy mittens

squishy lifebelt bouncer

Nautical Knitwear

Webbed booties

TRAFALGAR

boat blanket —
Nono and Mrs Baxter are
very patriotic —
apparently it's important
for Nappie to know that
his namesake was defeated
by Nelson who was British —
YAWN

Mrs Baxter thought
a pirate baby bag would be
a good idea

☆ some coats in some pretty wild stripy patterns
 ☆ a kind of all-in-one suit that had dangly bits from
the wrists and feet, for mittens and shoes to be attached to
 ☆ a whole load of things that any jaunty sailor would be
dead pleased to wear.

Nono told me that Melissa and Doug had decided to give
Napoleon a naming ceremony. I could tell that Nono thought

40

Napoleon was a strange name for a baby. Think she's right. I mean what kind of pathetic name is it? Everyone must realize that he's going to be called Nappie when he goes to school. It's bad enough that Nappie's got a dad like Doug. And a mum like Melissa, who will probably make all the poor kid's toys out of recycled yogurt pots and stuff she's found in the canal.

When Melissa and Doug got married they had their wedding on the Common. It was dead embarrassing with Melissa wearing one of her kind of cardigan outfits. I was a bridesmaid and had to wear a dress that made me look like one of those horrid orange boiled sweets you find down the back of the car seat. Apparently, Melissa thought it made me look like the sun. Yeh, right. I was like 'I'm sorry. Are you really expecting me to wear that?' Unfortunately, the answer was 'Yes'. But Xanthe helped me to sort it a bit and we kind of customized it. It was less disgusting when we finished with it – but not much.

Anyway, Nono said that Nappie's naming ceremony was not going to be on the Common. Instead it was going to be at the Community Centre where 'Dear Marcus' (that's my dad) is going to paint some of his pictures. IS MY FAMILY COMPLETELY OUT TO GET ME?

So I asked Nono what a naming ceremony actually was. I mean if we already know what Nappie's name is why do we need to be in the same place as all of Doug's matching relatives (everyone in his family looks exactly the same) to be told all over again?

Nono said she wasn't entirely sure what a naming ceremony was, but that she did know it didn't involve any

41

vicars and that 'Sweet Mary' (that's my mum) had kindly said she would write the words for the ceremony. Are they mad? This means that the words will be totally sick-making and embarrassing. My mum can only write things that rhyme – with words like 'bunny rabbits' and 'clouds' – things that you just don't want to hear. I thought I had it bad! Poor old Nappie has got it worse – and he's too young to realize it yet!

Nono also said that Melissa had told her that they were going to use crystals at the ceremony. Now we're talking! I'm thinking those crystals like you see on all the movie stars' clothes in HELLO! I'm thinking crystal-encrusted trainers and maybe a T-shirt or two? Or perhaps a dress! Nono will look fab in crystal earrings and matching hat.

Mrs Baxter said that she'd heard my dad talking with Doug in the garden. She said that they have decided to have home-made wine instead of home-made beer to 'wet the baby's head'. They'll drown it more like! Personally I would rather die than taste Dad and Doug's home-made beer — even if it was offered to me. They brewed nettle beer for the wedding, and it looked all sludgy. All the grown-ups (groan ups more like) drank so much they started to wobble. Then they started to giggle. It was just so embarrassing.

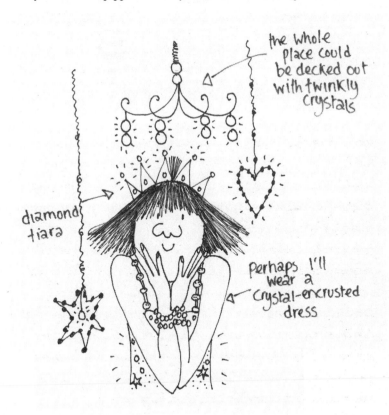

the whole place could be decked out with twinkly crystals

diamond tiara

perhaps I'll wear a crystal-encrusted dress

think this might be stuck on his head by now – bet he wears it in the bath

they've just strained this through one of Doug's old socks – EW!

it has to be Doug's sock because Dad never wears any

But Mrs Baxter said that she'd heard Dad saying that he'd got a bumper crop of courgettes on his allotment so he was going to make some wine with that. How gross is that?! Chateau Courgette! Probably complete with wriggling things. Cack!

At least Nono said that she was going to make the cake.

for Nappie's naming ceremony. Nappie Juice, in other words

Chateau Courgette
2005

Nothing else at the naming ceremony will be worth eating. It will be:

- brown
- hard
- tasteless
- gritty
- wet in the middle if it isn't completely hard.

But Nono said she had decided to make a three-layer cake. She's going to do a layer of chocolate, a layer of lemon and a layer of vanilla. And she's going to do that fluffy icing that's

think she's forgotten her knitting needles

he's ALL made of sugar

Nono had to stand on a stool to reach Napoleon's hat

Chocolate, lemon and vanilla

Napoleon

all soft and delish. And she's going to make a mini Napoleon out of sugar to stick on the top. Now that will be worth eating!

When we'd finished tea, I told Nono about Xanthe's new house. Nono was really brilliant with Xanthe when things were going badly with her mum and dad. She really likes Xanthe and said she and Mrs Baxter wanted to make a house warming present for her and Tasmin. They'd decided to knit something but didn't know what.

Mrs Baxter suggested:

☆ a set of matching cushion covers
☆ a cosy for their doorbell so that it doesn't freeze up in winter
☆ a mother-and-daughter set of bedsocks
☆ something more useful only she couldn't think what it could be.

We all decided that the doorbell thing was not right. And I managed to persuade them both that Xanthe and her mum had lots of cushion covers and wouldn't be cold enough to need bedsocks. We talked for ages about what would be good. And then Brian and one of Mrs Baxter's terriers (she'd brought the one that got on really well with Brian into the room with her) started barking like crazy when someone slammed a car door in the street.

Then Mrs B and Nono were off! 'That's it!' they both said. Tasmin and Xanthe didn't have a dog, did they? I thought, 'Oh no — they are going to give them a Baxter

Terrier!' But no! Nono knew that Tasmin and Xanthe wouldn't want a real dog. But they could have a knitted one.

Mrs B and Nono were totally off then, deciding which one of Mrs B's terriers to use as their life model. They were going to make the dog three-dimensional. And Nono reckoned she'd be able to find some kind of gizmo that would fit inside the dog so that it could bark at people in the hallway.

It was getting late. So I left them plotting their dog. Moi? I needed to get home to design my naming ceremony crystals.

 TEXT to Tarqs: U STL WIV GOB?

TEXT from Tarqs: YS

Poo!

FOOT AND MOUTH DISEASE

My mum and dad think that having a car that occasionally works means that you have a house full of modern gadgets and up-to-the minute cool and trendy stuff. Er, like NOT! We still have a telephone with a dial in our house — so fat chance of me being allowed to surf the Net and do my homework.

So next day, when we had Geography homework to do, I went back to Xanthe's house. It was looking dead cool — no skanky brown furniture there. I mean, Xanthe's mum and dad had had this brilliant house when they were still together. But even now they'd split up and Xanthe and her mum were living in this new house, it already looked like something out of a magazine.

Anyway, Xanthe's got this gorgeous laptop — it's all shimmery blue and scrummy. Her dad bought it for her. Like dads are meant to do. I mean, if I had a proper dad, you know, like a rock star with loads of dosh who cared enough about his

daughter to buy her heaps of stuff with it, then I would have a blue laptop too. I would also have:

✩ a lifetime subscription to Vogue, Cosmo Girl, Elle Girl, OK!, Hello! – and everything else I fancy in the shop
✩ all the clothes in Miss Sixty
✩ all the clothes in Prada
✩ real Armani jeans
✩ a converted attic bedroom with its own dressing room, shower room and jacuzzi
✩ £200 per week pocket money
✩ anything I fancy.

Only I haven't got a dad like that, have I? I've got a dad who for once in his life got some money and then decided that the only 'fair' thing (fair?!?!) he could do for society was to give all the money away. Der!

So, there I was at Xanthe's, surfing the Net looking for stuff about the world's climate. Yawn, yawn. We found loads of sites that gave us the answers to our homework so it didn't really take that long. Then Xanthe suggested that we do the actual homework on the laptop too, as a kind of joint project. Ha ha! It sounded good to me so Xanthe said she'd go downstairs and find us something to scoff while we did it. Even better!

I stayed upstairs and was just about to get out of the search engine when I found this link. You see we'd been looking up about the cold climates in the world. I saw this site called the National Cold Centre. Like what kind of stupid country is going to have a dumb place where everyone gets together to talk about it being cold? Or maybe, I thought, this was a place where it was extra specially cold? I clicked the site name to find out.

Completely weird! It wasn't anything to do with the climate – it was some place in the country where people go to catch a cold – on purpose! I'm sorry? Why would anyone want to get a cold? Seriously, people go for a week to get a bunged-up nose. Snot! Slime! They have Cold Holidays. Lovely. I mean, like how sad is that?

I tried to imagine the kind of people who went on holiday to catch a cold:

 ☻ drippy people (obviously)
 ☻ saddos
 ☻ people who haven't got any friends who'd want to go with them to somewhere sunny and groovy
 ☻ in other words, I suddenly realized, people like Hugo! Natch!

There was a place on the site where you could download a form to apply for the chance to go to the National Cold Centre for a week to help them with their research. I had to have one! After all, if Hugo's really serious about being some conservation guru, I reckoned he'd need to do his bit to help conserve his germs at the National Cold Centre. Easy peasy, I pressed the button and the form came out of the printer. I decided that I'd fill it in for him later. It'd be a pleasure!

My friend Xanthe is great because:

☆ she's my friend even if I'm in a bad mood
☆ she's still my mate when I sound like a dork
☆ she never loses her temper
☆ she's dead cool
☆ she makes me happy when I'm feeling sad.

I was on my way home from Xanthe's when I saw Tarquin coming out of our coal-hole. Wow — he looked mega-cool in his roadie gear. How could I ever have fancied Shoe Puke Jake? There is no way he is as gorgeous as MY BOYFRIEND Tarquin.

I did not want Tarqs to see me looking all skanky in my school uniform. (OK, I know that he sees me every day in my school uniform, but this was after school, and I reckoned there was a chance that we could be on our way to a second date.) So I whizzed back to the corner shop and tried to look as if I was looking at the ads in the window — you know, the ones that people write on those tatty postcards to advertise their disgusting last year's Christmas presents for sale? Like they think someone else would want their minging hat and scarf sets? NOT!

Anyway, what I was really doing in the shop window was trying to see my reflection in the window. So I:

☆ did a mega-quick hair change

☆ pinched my cheeks to get an LA glow

☆ bit my lips to give them some colour, then licked them to make them shine

☆ hitched my skirt up even higher to show off my looooooong legs.

(Another reason why Xanthe is my best friend is because she taught me all these tricks to make me look fabbo!)

The only problem was that while I was doing all this in the shop window, Mr Patel kept on waving at me from the other side. You see he thought I was looking for something. It was dead embarrassing because I didn't want to ignore him because he's dead nice. But then I didn't want him to see me doing my beauty stuff either! So I waved back. Only I dropped my school bag on the floor, and everything fell out of it. And now all my school stuff was covered in dirty fluff and bits of chewing gum!

I grabbed everything and shoved it back in my bag. Then, trying to look cool and doing the catwalk swagger that Xanthe and I have practised, I shimmied up to Tarqs. He said

flutter eyelashes to make eyes dewy and irresistible

grab school tie and whizz up over hair creating stunning tousled look

bite lips to make them lippy red and do film star style smile

undo top two buttons and hope vest doesn't show

Instant transformation technique

rolled-up school skirt (always wear school skirt this way - naturally)

hello and gave me his drop-dead gorgeous smile. I tried to open my mouth and say something cool back, but I just ended up saying hello because I couldn't think of anything else to say. Tarqs is TO DIE FOR!

But there was this terrible noise coming from the coal-hole. It was GOB rehearsing. I could hear Ben groaning his 'I don't want to get out of bed' routine as he bashed his drums,

moi looking like I've just stepped out of Fame Academy — can't actually think of much to say but looking gorgeous

MY BOYFRIEND!!

and I think Jake was playing his guitar only it sounded like he was strangling a cat. Der-brain (that's the other nerd in GOB that no one has ever been introduced to) was torturing his guitar too.

Next door, Mrs Baxter's dogs were howling. Actually, I reckoned they made a better noise than GOB. But they were still pretty awful. Anyway, the dogs were at the windows, howling away, and GOB were downstairs moaning and groaning. And there was me and Tarqs trying to be all romantic on the pavement.

NOT! Because just then one of Mrs B's dogs appeared on the pavement and started sniffing around at my bag which was by my feet. I tried to push it away, but I suppose the stink from the pavement outside the shop must have been delish to a Baxter. Because it lifted its leg up and started to do a wee.

look! He's AMAZED by my beauty

A great big long hot one. I know it was a great big long hot one. How do I know? Because it did it up my leg and all over my shoe! I had dog wee all over my leg. And all over my school bag. And all over my shoe.

Tarquin just looked at me. Then he said, 'What is it about your feet?' And I looked at him and said 'I think I'd better go.'

'Yeah — see you!' Tarquin said.

I squelched away. A hot squelch. Some second date.

Tarquin was right. I mean, WHY'S EVERYONE GOT IT IN FOR MY FEET?

TEXT from Tarqs: U DRID UR FT YT?

TEXT to Tarqs: WOT U THNK!

Honestly, boys . . .

I HATE dogs
AND
I HATE my brothers
AND
I HATE GOB
AND
I HATE this STUPID
MUSIC

MY BROTHER STINKS!

I had to wear trainers to school the next day. I told Mum that she'd have to buy me a new pair of school shoes on account of the wee situation. But she said they would 'clean up nicely'. Like right! No way am I going to wear those shoes again.

I think Mum should buy me some shoes that are:

☆ *high enough to make me over five foot seven*
☆ *pointy-toed*

fabby toes

scrumptious

my kinda shoes

beautiful bo

☆ kitten-heeled
☆ probably black with white highlights.

They should definitely NOT have:

lappy toes →

← sensible

boring bows

mum's kinda shoes

♀ sensible heels
♀ laces
♀ room to grow into
♀ the school-shoe look that all mums like.

I told Xanthe all about it the next day at school. I had to wait until lunchtime to tell her, though, because I couldn't tell her something like that on the bus, and I'm not good enough at text messages yet to tell her everything that happened.

So, we were sitting at lunchtime in the school canteen. It was Caribbean Calypso day in what they laughingly call the

School Restaurant. So all the dinner ladies and the school cook were dressed up in African national dress. They were playing background music too. The music and the food were OK (ANY food is better than the cack that my parents cook) but the clothes were pants.

Anyway, I was sitting with Xanthe and we were talking about what we were going to wear for the naming ceremony. Xanthe said that her mum had loads of crystals at home that she used for her jewellery, and she'd said she would help us to make our outfits. Bless! But the only thing we had with us at lunchtime was the pen in our pockets. So we grabbed some napkins from the buffet counter and used them to do our designs.

don't know what he thinks he's looking at — freak

Xanthe actually LIKES dead fish

one of my many fabulous frock ideas

dead fish — UGH, but the rest was OK

I fancied:

☆ loads of crystals dangling down to catch the light
☆ something slinky
☆ something dead sophisticated to suit my personality
☆ a dress that would make Tarquin's eyes pop out.

So between us, Xanthe and I came up with this halter neck:

our final design for my crystal-encrusted
'naming ceremony' dress

Xanthe said she wanted her dress to look very simple so that she could wear it with lots of her mum's jewellery and show that off. She thought maybe a polo-neck dress like this:

her dress was going to be black but the felt-tip pen ran out

Xanthe

says she might pad her bottom for that J-Lo look

Xanthe's dress is going to be totally elegant with loads of sparkly jewellery

We'd just about finished when the end-of-lunch bell went. Xanthe was going to take the designs home to show her mum, and then we were going to get together to make them up.

What would I do if I didn't have a brillo friend like Xanthe?

I went straight home on my own after school that day.

Mum and Dad were at the Community Centre. They'd left a note on the kitchen table to say they were getting things ready for the naming ceremony. But that was ages away! And how much was there to get ready anyway? Mum's note said that Ben was 'babysitting' for me and Hugo! What! Like I'm a baby now, am I? Like NOT!

Still, at least Ben's idea of babysitting was doing just what he normally did. Which was being down in the cellar and making the usual racket that GOB make when they are rehearsing.

Just outside our kitchen there's a door going down to the cellar. So I stuck my head down there to see if Tarquin was doing his roadie bit with GOB. I wasn't surprised that he wasn't there – I hadn't seen him on the bus after all. But I did wonder what he was up to! What is it with boys that they are never where you want them, when you want them?

I went back into the kitchen to see if there was anything to scoff in the fridge. Surprise, surprise, there was nothing. At Nono's house the fridge would be bursting its doors with delish things. At our house, it was full of:

 ❦ brown things
 ❦ brown things with green things stuck to them
 ❦ plates that were empty
 ❦ other things that had perhaps once been food but

now looked like those weird hairy cactuses you see in the windows of flats where old ladies who are loads older than Nono live.

Won't risk eating the green bits

these brown bits might have been chocolate once

BISCUITS ← well, that's a joke — should say ' broken mouldy bits and crumbs!

Eventually I found some biscuit things in a tin in the cupboard. They were really hard and heavy going. But at least they had some kind of sugar in them. I was munching on my second one when Hugo came in to the kitchen. He said, 'Hello, sister!' in his puke-making sucky-uppy way and started to search around in the cupboards too.

So, being dead sisterly and kind, I said, 'The only thing worth eating is these — here.' And I offered him one of the biscuits. But Hugo said, 'Oh no, sister dear. I'm not looking for a biscuit, I'm looking for containers — like these!' He grabbed some old jars and boxes and then disappeared into the garden.

MY BROTHER IS COMPLETELY WEIRD. But then I always knew that — from the minute he was born I knew he looked bonkers and nothing like the babies my other friends at nursery had as their brothers and sisters. That's why I asked

66

Nono if she could put him in the gutter one day and leave him there. But, of course, Nono just said, 'No, no, Amaryllis darling, we can't do that. Here, have a lovely drop scone instead.'

Anyway, that was then, this is now. Back in the kitchen, I was bored. I sent a text to Xanthe:

 TEXT to Xanthe: FNCE CMN RND?

But she sent one back saying:

 TEXT from Xanthe: CNT — WIV DAD!

So that was that. We haven't got a telly so I couldn't watch that. And I couldn't talk to Tarquin about it because, being a boy, he Just Wouldn't Understand. And I couldn't go round to Nono's because she was taking Mrs Baxter out in her sports car. They were going to be in the audience of Countdown, their fave telly prog.

There was no way I was going to do my homework like some kind of swot. So the only thing that was left to do was find out what Hugo was up to in the garden. It had been raining while we were at school, so the garden path was even more slimy than normal. That didn't seem to bother Hugo, though. He was on his hands and knees saying things like 'Gorgeous specimen!' and 'Excellent' as he grabbed things and put them into the jars and stuff he'd taken from the kitchen.

I asked him what he was doing. He looked all smug and said, 'My slug survey!' and disappeared into the shed.

The garden shed is another thing in our house that IS SO NOT FAIR! Because Hugo, being the slimy creep that he is, *spends so much time in the garden that Dad decided he was a budding gardener. (Hugo made — pass the sick bag — a Wormery last summer. Yes, a place where he keeps worms — ON PURPOSE. He's also got a compost heap that Mum thinks*

is just SOOOO clever because it recycles all the dead food in our house. Creep!) So Dad said he could have the garden shed as his own little den! Per-lease! Like anyone said I could have a den – NOT! The fact that I do not like to do any gardening has nothing to do with it! I mean, I could have a disco den in the shed, couldn't I?

Until this particular moment, I had never been remotely interested in seeing what Hugo got up to in his smelly little garden home. But I had nothing better to do, and Hugo had left the door open, so I followed him in.

FER-EEEAA-KEY OR WHAT!

Hugo had got all these slimy slugs slurping their way round the jars and boxes on the shelves. There were some spiders too. And on the walls, he's stuck up all these posters of animals and insects. There was a pile of old magazines in the corner called THE COMPLETE COMPOSTER. But the really

scary thing was all the mirrors that Hugo had put up in the shed. As I stood there gobsmacked in the doorway, I could see that every time Hugo walked past one of the mirrors, he looked into it and smiled at himself. CHEESY! The little creep was practising his 'I'm-going-to-be-a-telly-presenter-of-hairy-and-slimy-things' smiles.

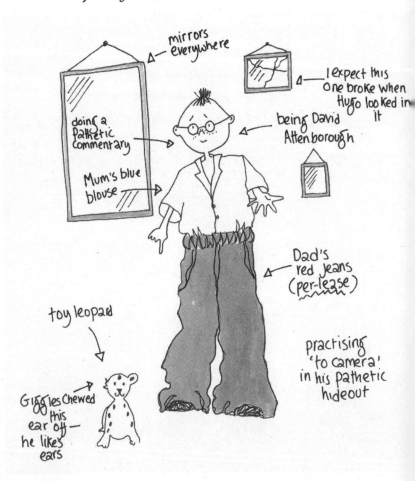

mirrors everywhere

I expect this one broke when Hugo looked in it

doing a pathetic commentary

being David Attenborough

Mum's blue blouse

Dad's red jeans (per-lease)

toy leopard

practising 'to camera' in his pathetic hideout

Giggles chewed this ear off — he likes ears

DEE-SGUST-ING!

That was it! Enough! I went to my room and filled in the form for the Cold Research Centre. If Hugo wanted to be famous at doing research into all things natural, what would be more natural than catching a cold?

I'm going to have 'Kiss curls' in the morning

MY BOYFRIEND

dreaming about Hugo being eaten by a giant slug

TEXT to Xanthe: U WLL NT BLEV WOT MY BRUV IS UP 2!

TEXT from Xanthe: CLL U L8R!

WHO NEEDS ENEMIES WHEN YOU'VE GOT RELLIES LIKE MINE?

I posted the form on my way to school the next morning. Xanthe couldn't believe I'd actually done it when I told her about it. She said she thought I was really mean. But then I said she hadn't even got one brother let alone two brothers, one of which was Hugo, so she didn't know just how desperate a girl could get.

Told her all about his disgusting little Hugo slime den when we were walking to her house after school. When I told her about the mirrors, she said maybe he was a bit of a worry. I said, 'Who cares about him?' and when we got to hers we forgot all about it because her mum had all these fabby things laid out on her kitchen table for us. She was going to help us with our dresses, with the crystals and stuff!

Tasmin is just SO clever. She'd got all this material and she sort of draped it over us and then snipped away with some scissors. She showed me and Xanthe how to use her dinky little sewing machine, and then we zapped away with it, sewing the pieces together. It was just MEGA! I loved it. Now I want a sewing machine too!

Why isn't my mum brilliant at something?

Why doesn't my mum have gorgeous clothes?

Why doesn't my mum have amazing shoes?

Cool

Why isn't Tasmin MY MUM?

The crystals were brill too! I kind of threaded loads on to a string of the fabric and sewed some down the back of the dress too. It was brill! Xanthe was threading her crystals on to jewellery wire and making all these gorgeous bracelets and necklaces. FAB!

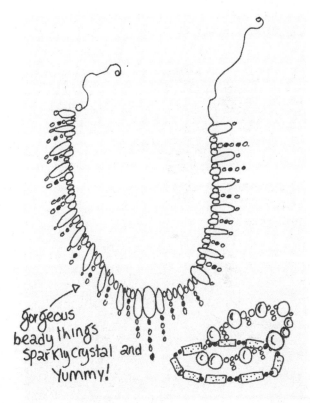

gorgeous beady things sparkly crystal and yummy!

And Tasmin was helping us all the time. I said to her, 'You're so quick at this and so brill at this — you should have a shop!'

Was having such a good time I didn't want to leave.

But it was Baking Day at Nono's so I decided that maybe I should pop in on her on my way home to check things out. Nono told me all about being in the telly studio with Mrs Baxter as I scoffed on the banana bread and then some coffee and walnut cake. Then she showed me the hat that she'd knitted to wear to the naming ceremony. There was a pair of socks for Mrs Baxter too.

    Nono is just amazing with her knitting needles.
    But it was getting late so I had to go home.
    BIG MISTAKE!

Melissa was there with Doug and Nappie.

It gets worse.

Dad and Doug were practising something called Morris dancing in the kitchen. Apparently they are going to do this dance at the naming ceremony to celebrate the world for Nappie. Don't know who this Morris bloke is but he is PANTS at dancing. And so are Dad and Doug. Embarrassing or what?

Ben was playing the bongo drums for them to dance to. I suppose it makes a change for him to be out in daylight.

And I suppose you've got to give him credit for being better at the drums than Dad and Doug are at dancing. I mean, per-lease! They kept waving tea towels in the air as they danced.

HEALTH ALERT—
barefoot overdose....

don't look unless
you want to THROW UP

Left the kitchen sharpish. The living room was even worse! Mum was at one end reciting her words. Melissa and Doug have asked her to write the ceremony. That should be enough to make everyone choke on their onion and grit bajees.

you can tell she's getting all emotional because her earrings are flapping around

MARY'S MOMENT

Xanthe's mum would never wear spots with stripes

these are the sad sort of shoes that m loves

DING-A-LING

Melissa

Melissa was at the other end of the living room tinging these hand bells around with this glazed 'Gosh I'm Dead Clever' look in her eyes. Gosh-I'm-A-Complete-Loony more like.

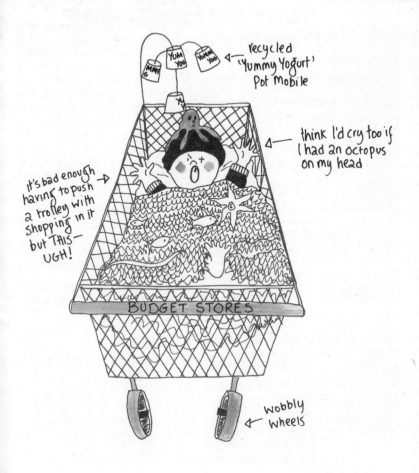

recycled 'Yummy Yogurt' Pot Mobile

think I'd cry too if I had an octopus on my head

It's bad enough having to push a trolley with shopping in it but THIS — UGH!

BUDGET STORES

Wobbly Wheels

Nappie was in his pram screaming his head off! It was awful. But I suppose the only good thing is that perhaps it shows Nappie's got more sense and realizes that his entire family (except MOI!) are nutty as fruitcakes.

Mum said, 'Oh dear, Napoleon's crying! Perhaps he needs a walk?'

81

So I said, 'I'll take him!'
Anything to get out of the
Nut House!

But when I got
into the hall, I realized
that taking Nappie out
for a walk in his pram-
shopping trolley thingy
meant that people I
knew might see me doing
it! They might realize that I was
actually related to him and, what's WORSE, to
his parents! Did some double-quick thinking
and grabbed a pair of sunglasses from the hall
table. Think they must be Hugo's I'm-going-to-be-
famous glasses. Saw how gorgeous I looked in them in the hall

it better not
UP CHUCK ON
my T-shirt

Moi, travelling incogn
had to pinch
Hugo's shades

recycled carrier
bag sunshade

trying really hard
not to get too
close

Xanthe
bag

why doesn't
it stop
squawking?

mirror, pulled Nappie's hat down as low as I could and shoved him out of the door.

Thought that I'd practise my slinky halter-neck-dress walk as I walked up and down the street. Nappie was staring at me from the pram so I guess I got it right. I could almost begin to like him! Was just coming up the other side of the road when DISASTER! The GOB van pulled up. They were coming to our house for a rehearsal. And the first person out of the van was Tarquin.

And he saw me pushing a baby in a pram.

Like do I actually have to say how TOTALLY embarrassing that was? And how come Tarquin was tipping up now? Where had he been? ... Like I said, why are boys never in the right place at the right time?

 TEXT to Xanthe: AM DED!

TEXT from Xanthe: LTS TLK!

WEE AND HUMILIATION – BOTH IN ONE DAY

The actual naming ceremony was at the weekend. It was a
Total World Humiliation Event because the local council had
decided to unveil the fact that:

    ☠ my dad had GIVEN AWAY ALL HIS MONEY
    ☠ yhey had decided to call the Community Centre
after him
    ☠ there was going to be this bloke Morris dancing.

So they'd got the local telly people in and the local paper too! I
got changed at Xanthe's house. Natch, we looked gorgeous.
BUT! We hadn't thought about what we were going to put on
over our crystal creations to get to the Community Centre. And
it was C-O-L-D!

85

We reckoned that we could take our tops off when we got there, and no one would know. So we grabbed our fleeces, zipped up and got to the Community Hall. Nono was just getting out of her car with Mrs Baxter when we arrived. She'd even knitted a crystal collar for Brian to wear. He looked loads better than Doug and the Dougalikes. They were looking like they always did really. A bit freaky and dead boring.

There were cameras everywhere, so we shimmied across the road to the Hall and shoved our fleeces in the hedge.

Me and Xanthe realized that the bloke with the camera was pointing the thing in our direction. He had followed us across the road!

And he was still looking at us now. Thought it must have been because of our mega-gorgeous looks and clothes. We took a deep breath and let our crystals shimmer in the camera. Did my catwalk and strutted over to the tarmac in front of Xanthe. But she suddenly grabbed me and said, 'Quick!' and pushed me into a hedge to join the fleeces.

Now I NEVER normally get angry with Xanthe, but this time I did. 'Like what did you do that for?' I hissed.

And she said, 'Because your knickers are showing at the back!'

My face went so red I thought I'd melt! I groped around the back of me, trying to find where my knicks were caught up in the dress. But they weren't caught up in my dress! IT WAS WORSE THAN THAT! The halter neck was so low at the back that the mega knickers that my mum always buys me were sticking up to my waist.

I've shrugged off my fleece à la top model

Now I knew why the camera bloke was interested in us walking across the road! He was just a great big knob of cheese.

I couldn't bear it. Xanthe went back to grab our fleeces, but they were covered in loads of cacky rubbish and sticky bits. We put them on — I suppose it was going to be

better wearing that than showing my knickers. But not the same as looking like Beyoncé.

Had to stand feeling like a twit as some council bloke in seriously dodgy shoes and a big tacky necklace yawned on about how mega-wonderful my dad was (well he would be, wouldn't he, if he'd given the council loads of money?) and what a great pleasure it was to unveil this fantastic piece of community art for everyone on this ultra-special occasion. Then Dad pulled this string that was attached to this grey material from the front of the Community Hall.

Tasmin would never make anything as uncool as this

the only interesting thing about him is that his chin wobbles when he talks

tan suede

about to unveil the painting

mum's wearing chandeliers

SLOB

Little creep wearing shades and a frilly collar that Nono knitted

Nono's telling Ben not to pick his pimples

Yawn, yawn . . . Then second world humiliation time, here we come. Because when the grey stuff came down, it revealed exactly what my dad had been up to when he was spending all that time down at the Hall over the last few weeks. He'd been doing a painting. A mural to be precise. OK — so I knew that Dad was doing a mural and it was going to be ALL over the walls and it was going to feature all of us.

BUT I MEAN, HOW COULD MY DAD DO THAT TO ME? A DIRTY GREAT PICTURE OF ME ABOUT THREE METRES TALL IN A SMOCKED DRESS STANDING NEXT TO ALL MY FAMILY, LOOKING LIKE A GEEK.

And there is more! The Community Hall is now called The Flowerdew Drop In — as in Do/Dew Drop In. Like that's meant to be funny?

Only good thing was that Melissa said the telly cameras and the press weren't allowed in to the naming ceremony because she said she wanted Nappie to be Clean and Pure. Has she seen what he does in his nappies?

But at least the bloke with the camera couldn't come in. Everyone bundled inside and Melissa told us all to gather round in a circle so that we could 'close the life force'. Per-lease!

Then when everyone was standing round my mum

started the whole thing off with one of her cringey poems. It went something like this:

> Here today and still tomorrow
> Lots of joy and never sorrow
> Napoleon's the baby
> Who might join the navy (might have hair wavy?)
> He's small and he's great
> He's gained lots of weight!
> Let's celebrate
> And make a state-
> Ment that the baby Napoleon
> Is the one we are calling on
> To go forth in the world
> And make us all proud.

hope she doesn't knock herself out

She's go to read WHOLE B of stu

Desperate or what? But, of course, it got more desperate.
Because after that it wasn't just Dad and Doug that started
waving their bells in the air. HUGO JOINED IN TOO! And
then the Dougalikes decided that they would have a go.

93

Nono kept shaking her head and saying, 'No, no.' Then she went with Mrs Baxter to the table where she'd laid out all her food at one end. Xanthe and me followed her. If we had to endure this naming thing then at least we could eat the best food before everyone else got to it.

being a superstar → makes you very hungry

choccy blobs on top ▷

Nono's nosh ▷

I was scoffing on an iced bun when Melissa started her bit. Nappie lay mesmerized on a blanket while his mum waved these crystals over him and tinged her bells. The poor kid was completely naked, and Melissa explained to everyone that he came into the world with nothing, and now with nothing he was being given his name. Like HELLO?

Hugo was, of course, all mega sucky uppy. Still glowing from his Morris dancing, he was right up close to Nappie and going all goo goo, ga ga in his face at him. Everyone was going, 'Isn't he so sweet, the way he loves the baby!'

Xanthe and me were going, 'Isn't he so pukey?' at the back.

But result!

Hugo was just getting all coochy-coo with Nappie at the end of the bell ringing when YES! Nappie did a wee! I didn't know little boy babies could wee so high. And all over Hugo too!

HA HA, VERY FUNNY! HUGO'S NAME IS BUGS BUNNY!

That's Bugs Bunny WITH WEE IN HIS EYE!

After that it all got a bit boring. Until Tarquin sent me a text. It said:

TEXT from Tarqs: CN I C U 2NITE?

Like he had to ask?

YESSSS!

DATES AND DER-BRAINS

I sent Tarqs a text back asking him where we were going. He sent one back saying: SKOOL. Like, I'm sorry? Here was me thinking we were going to some posh frock place and all he wanted to do was see me at school on Monday! So I sent him another text saying: WOT?

It wasn't till he sent me another text telling me that GOB were doing a gig at school that I realized that he still meant he wanted to see me tonight. Relief or what?

Xanthe said, 'D'you want me to help you get ready?'

'Per-lease!' I said.

So I went off to check with my mum that it was OK. But she was so busy doing her rhyming stuff and giggling in the way that grown-ups do when they are at parties — honestly, they behave like kids! — that I don't think she took on board what I was saying. So I thought I'd go and find Dad and tell him, you know, just in case they suddenly wondered where

I was in a couple of hours' time. That was a waste of time too — because Dad was discussing the finer art of Morris dancing with a Dougalike and didn't seem to take much notice. How desperate can my parents get?

I went over to Nono and told her. She smiled at me and said, 'No, no, darling — have a lovely time, my sweet, won't you? Bye bye, Amaryllis. Bye bye, Xanthe.'

So we legged it back to Xanthe's. We decided that the dress — the dress — was not remotely suitable for a GOB gig. Xanthe is the best of best friends because she just said, 'We'll find something' and whizzed open her wardrobe. Of course, coming from an artistic family, Xanthe has a wardrobe that is

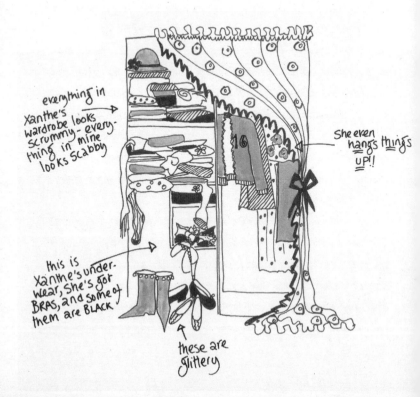

everything in Xanthe's wardrobe looks scrummy — everything in mine looks scabby

She even hangs things up!!

this is Xanthe's underwear, she's got BRAS, and some of them are BLACK

these are glittery

covered with a shimmery silk and bead curtain, full of fabby things. She's got:

- ☆ at least three pairs of bootleg jeans
- ☆ some to-die-for boots with bells on
- ☆ a bright pink satin baseball jacket
- ☆ a really, really short skirt in leopard print
- ☆ a jumper with shimmery beads on it
- ☆ an army shirt.

I, on the other hand, have a disgusting chest of drawers and a rather tatty cardboard thing that my dad says is an ethically correct wardrobe for the twenty-first century – huh! – and in it are:

- ♀ the disgusting rain cape that my mum bought me from America (I tried to throw it away but my mum found it in the compost bin and thought it was in there by 'accident')
- ♀ a selection of items that my mum tie-dyed using old tea bags
- ♀ another selection of things that Melissa dyed with some weeds she found on the canal bank
- ♀ things that my Mum thinks are suitable for my age – per-lease!
- ☆ a couple of decent jumpers made by Nono.

Anyway, Xanthe took out some rather scrummy leggings made of this stuff that looks like velvet. She said they would look good

looks sort of boring

Xanthe's leggings are a bit short on me

the most gorgeous chair, all shocking pink and gold

with the trainers that I'd sewn loads of sequins on. But we couldn't think what I should wear on top — until we had an idea to jazz up a T-shirt.

Tasmin lent us all these amazing fabric pens. All we had to do was use them just like ordinary felt pens to write and draw all over a bog-standard T-shirt. Then we used this fabric glue and sprinkled some sequins and glitter in a few discreet places. Result? A customized T-shirt! Good result! And it was dead easy to make — quick too. So quick that we made a couple and couldn't decide which one I should wear.

Tarquin has asked me to meet him at school because, of course, he was doing all his roadie stuff for the gig. So I

asked Xanthe if she would come
with me to the gig. Then
she could wear the
other T-shirt that I
didn't wear! At
first she didn't
want to come
because she said
she didn't want to
tag along to my
date. But to be
honest I wasn't sure
that I wanted to be
alone on my date with
Tarquin. Although could I
be alone on a date that was a
gig full of headbangers? Course I wanted Xanthe to come!

can't wait to get
her mitts on my
T-shirt

scrummy sparkly
bits and
paints and
Pens

this table's pink
and gold too...

this is
almost a bra

We had to
put newspaper
in the T-shirt
so the paint
didn't go through

it's going to
be so fab

So we did our make-up — just a tiny bit of mascara and some lip gloss. And a bit of blusher and some hair make-up. Oh, and some body art and a hint of blusher. Very natural. Then we were off to catch the bus to school.

ready to Rock

Xanthe lent me her beads

CutiePie

sugar plum!

We cut off the bottom and stuck on some sparkly bits

stuck sequins on my tummy

rolled the leggings up to look totally cool

The bloke on the bus made us pay full fare! It was so not fair that fare! He said we couldn't be half fare because we had so much make-up on! We said, 'Look here, buster, we are only thirteen!'

And he said, 'Then why have you got so much warpaint on then?' And he laughed!

Oh, ha ha! Saddo! But then as Xanthe said, if he thought we had to pay full fare, we obviously looked dead old and sophis.

When we got to the stop outside school, we couldn't believe it. There were loads of people queuing up to go into school. There was a big banner across the gates saying, 'School Reunion Nite'. It was for all the really old people who used to go to our school years ago. They think that 'Nite' is a really witty joke. Per-lease!

I was a bit shocked to realize that GOB were going to play in front of so many people. I mean, I didn't realize that anyone was actually prepared to hear my brother and his mates doing their version of music. I suppose it takes all sorts.

But double-shocker! When Xanthe and I went through the gates into the hall, we bumped into Ms Pretty! Ms Pretty, our most favouritest teacher that we love to death. Fortunately, Ms Pretty still has absolutely no idea that it was Dad's parrot Frank that did the mega-parrot-poo down her back when she came to visit his shop once. It was the time that Tarquin was left running the shop when Mum and Dad were in America Being Famous. It is dead sad though, because Ms Pretty has told us that she is going to be leaving our school at the end of term. How pooey is that? The only decent teacher in school and she goes and leaves? Anyway, I said, 'Ms Pretty, what are you doing here?'

And she explained to us that she had organized the gig. So I said, 'But do you realize who GOB are?'

And she said that she did, and she thought they were fab, and I must be really proud of my brother and excited about the telly competition that they were in the final of. I think she was serious because Ms Pretty is too gorgeous to make fun out of me and Xanthe.

Anyway, then Ms Pretty said, 'I love your outfits, girls!' before she rushed off to make some welcome speech.

Well! Xanthe and I were standing there gobsmacked (this is NOT a joke) when I saw Tarquin. And he looked like some kind of god of gorgeousness! So I went over to where he was – not too fast but not too slow so that he didn't think I was too keen or not interested. I spent the rest of the evening following him around and helping him out. Xanthe did a bit too – but she also helped Ms Pretty with some stuff.

104

I was beginning to get a bit suspicious. I mean, if someone like Ms Pretty thought GOB were worth listening to, and so did a telly programme, perhaps they were worth more than our cellar. But I did have to remember that it was my brother who was their lead singer. And that one of their songs is called 'I don't

they lo
so coo

don't expect my mum even → knows that clothes like this EXIST

UGH!!

looks like he should live under a stone

BOG OFF

used to think this jersey was fridgey cool - now I know he wears it all the time, it must really pong

mega creep

Well I s'pose they might sound quite good, but they look GROSS

want to get out of bed'. During the gig, I discovered that their other songs were 'My chips've gone cold', 'Has anyone else got the tea bag?', 'I saw it in the fridge' and 'My dog's a space hero' – as if!

When it was all over, Xanthe's mum came to get us. But Tarquin said that I could go back in the GOB van with him, Ben and the other unmentionables. After all, we were going back to my house. So I said bye and thanks to Xanthe and helped Tarqs put some of the gear in the van. I made sure that my feet didn't go anywhere near Jake – or any other part of my anatomy, for that matter! Tarquin's hand kept touching mine as we put things in the van! Sweet!

The bad news, though, was when I realized that I had agreed to go home in a van — and a van only has two seats, and Ben was driving it with Jake sitting next to him. That was the good news — that I wouldn't be sitting next to Puke Man. But the worst news was that I would have to squeeze into the back with no-speak Der-brain as well as all the GOB kit. At least, though, I had Tarqs with me. And that made me forget about all the cack that was on the floor of the van that I was having to sit on.

I leaned on Tarqs all the way home. When we went round a really sharp corner I had to lean on him quite hard. Then when we got home, he helped me get out. We had an almost-kiss situation! And this time there was no dribble or spitty stuff!

If GOB hadn't been there, it probably would have been a proper kiss . . .

how can he *not* kiss me ??

 TEXT to Xanthe: GES WOT!

TEA CAKES, LACE
AND MS PRETTY

Dad said it was my turn to walk Giggles on Sunday afternoon. I hate walking him because he is so embarrassing. He spends hours sniffing every lamp post — and on top of that Dad says I have to pick up all his poos in one of his shop bags. It wouldn't be quite so bad if Dad's shop bags weren't made of recycled paper that goes soggy — eeuueeeugh!

I called Xanthe to ask her what she was up to. I didn't want to call Tarquin because I didn't want to look as if I wanted to see him. He might get the wrong idea! Xanthe said she wasn't up to much so she'd come out with me and Giggles. We met up at the end of the road and decided that we'd walk to Nono's. After all, Nono always lets Giggles come in — and more importantly she would have something delicious to eat. Probably with chocolate and icing on it.

Isn't this T-shirt just gorgeous? We painted glittery stars on to it

Giggles doesn't seem to want to come

We didn't plan it but Xanthe and I were both wearing our GOB gig T-shirts. Nono said 'No, no, girls — don't they look gorgeous.' Nono always knows how to make us feel great. Xanthe said thanks, but that she thought they could still do with a bit more on the bottom — maybe some kind of fringing.

CAKE!

BUNS!

SAND-WICHES

wearing her knitting specs

choccy icing

muffins

mooing mobile

remote control for vibrating chair

all sorts of different wool

Brian

And Nono said, what you girls need is some lace. She was right! 'But how could we afford lace?' I said. So Nono said she could knit some.

'Here girls, have some of this chocolate double-iced muffin cake while I do some knitted lace for you now.'

So we scoffed and Nono knitted. I may be unlucky enough to have ended up with a family of basket cases but I have got the granny of the century with Nono. Not only can she bake the best cakes but she can knit brill things too! And really quickly. She knitted so fast that she finished two lots of lace before we left. Then she found some sewing cotton and we were able to trim our T-shirts with the lace before we left. Did we look the business? Natch!

practising our model walks

sparkly scarves knitted by Nono

Nono's amazing knitted lace

can't he ever do anything right?

full of yummies from Nono

As we were leaving, gorgeous Nono said to wait a minute because she'd just remembered some other stuff she had for us. And she brought out these gorgeous scarves she'd made with fluffy wool. The fringes had all these lovely crystal beads threaded on them. There was one for Xanthe and another for me. Just perfect! Like Nono . . .

We went back to Xanthe's after that. I wasn't going to stay — just say hello to Tasmin and show her how we'd finished off the T-shirts with Nono's help. But Xanthe and I didn't reckon on finding Ms Pretty at Xanthe's! She was in the living room with Tasmin having tea out of these gorgeous teacups. In my house tea gets served in these disgusting chipped things that are just revolting and say things like 'Best Dad in the World' or (this one is my mum's and the revolting

doesn't look as if she's going to tell us off

scrummy beads

look at THESE-WOW!

saw this bag in a really posh shop in town

bead curtains

I knew! Should have done my maths homework

will probably wee on her wheel

there's only one person we know who has a zebra-striped Smart car

Hugo Poogo made it for her for Christmas once) 'I'm a poet and I didn't know it'. How about an 'Excuse me while I puke' mug?

Anyway, we knew Ms Pretty was in the house before we even opened the front door because we'd seen her car outside. You can't miss Ms Pretty's car. It is this stunning convertible Smart car, and everyone turns round at school when she turns up in it.

Tasmin and Ms Pretty were deep in conversation when we walked in. It was so embarrassing because as soon as we opened the door, Giggles trotted in and made this terrible noise and revolting smell. What is it with our animals and Ms Pretty? I hope Ms Pretty didn't think it was me! I grabbed Giggles's lead quick and took him back out to tie him to the gate. He immediately started to howl. Great. But he'd just have to wait.

I hissed at Giggles to be quiet — like he'd listen to me? — and went back inside. Xanthe and I looked at each other. After all, what was Ms Pretty doing there? And what were they so deeply in conversation about? What had we done wrong?

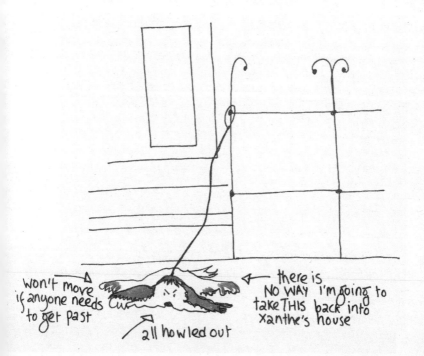

won't move if anyone needs to get past

all howled out

there is NO WAY I'm going to take THIS back into Xanthe's house

Tasmin spotted our lace on the T-shirts straightaway. My mum wouldn't have noticed it even if I'd got a big placard on my head saying LOOK DOWN AT THE GORGEOUS LACE ON AMARYLLIS'S CUSTOMIZED T-SHIRT! BY THE WAY, SHE DID IT HERSELF! Tasmin said, 'Wow!' and then turned to Ms Pretty and said, 'I told you these girls had talent.'

What did she mean? I could tell that Xanthe didn't

know either because she gave me the look that said what I was thinking. But before we could say anything Ms Pretty said, 'Where did you get those divine scarves, girls?'

I told her about Nono and Ms Pretty said, 'Well, if Xanthe gets her talent from her mother, then you obviously get yours from your gran.'

Obviously Ms Pretty knows what she is talking about. Tasmin asked us if we wanted some tea with them. To be honest I was stuffed with food and drink. But for the chance to sit down with Ms Pretty I was prepared to sacrifice myself. Only just at that moment, Giggles decided to howl so loudly that we actually thought there was a fire engine outside.

So I said, 'I think I'd better go, bye.'

Ms Pretty said she'd see me in school tomorrow and would look out for more of my sassy clothes. I could feel myself blushing and Xanthe gave me a hug.

I started planning how I was going to adapt my school uniform as soon as I shut the front door behind me.

 TEXT from Targs: CN I C U 2NITE?

TEXT to Targs: NO CHNC!

Like I was going to have time to be with him when a school uniform transformation situation was on the cards?

CAKES, CACK AND COLDS

Xanthe and I hung around in the school car park to say hello to Ms Pretty today. She smiled at us when she saw us! I'd hitched up my skirt and was wearing

my customized trainers. And I had some twizzly things in my hair. Xanthe was wearing her Nono scarf and some gloves that she'd put some fake fur cuffs on. Miss Pretty said, 'Love your outfits, girls!' and winked at us as we helped her get her bags from the boot of her car.

how come she didn't say anything about my twizzly bit

Apart from that it was a dead boring day at school. Except for

118

seeing Tarquin at lunchtime. Although he didn't say anything about my hair. And it took me half an hour before breakfast as well!

Xanthe had to go and see her dad after school. So I went to the library to see if I could find some books to give me ideas about textiles and stuff. Ways Xanthe and I could make more clothes look fab. I found some and then went straight home after that.

BIG MISTAKE! Because when I got there, I knew as soon as I opened the front door that something was up. I could hear voices. They were coming from the kitchen. And the kitchen was full of my family. Even Doug, Melissa and Nappie were there. The thing I didn't know was — why?

Mum greeted me like she hadn't seen me for about six years as soon as I walked into the room. So that was immediately suspicious! Everyone was giggling. Even Nappie was trying to laugh — perhaps he was laughing with hysterics because he's old enough now to realize what a bunch of pencil cases he's been born into. Poor old Nappie didn't look like he stood a chance with this lot. He already looked horribly like Doug — only with a touch of Melissa's recycled look.

Hugo was sitting at one end of the kitchen table looking even more smug than usual. He was obviously the reason that we were in the kitchen. I noticed that Mum had made a cake — always an event to avoid. Trust my luck to have the only mum in the world that doesn't know

a) how to make a cake

and

b) can't realize that she can't and doesn't go out and buy one from a shop!

Instead she still tries to make one. My mum's cakes are always:

mum's rea pleased her cake

...ar this

Poogo's nose will look just like the cherry after his 'prize'!!

🍭 heavy
🍭 grey-looking
🍭 like chewing on a brick.

This cake had even been decorated — with a kind of sludge-coloured icing and she'd put a cherry on the top.

Just after I arrived, Dad disappeared into the garden and then came back carrying two bottles. He had pink cheeks and was giggling like he did at the naming ceremony. Straightaway I realized why all the adults were so jolly — they'd been drinking Dad's nettle beer again. After he'd put the bottles down, Dad leaned over to Hugo and said, 'Well done, son!' Hugo just grinned back and said, 'Thanks, Dad' and smiled even more. Then he caught his reflection in the

kitchen window and patted down his hair, smiling at his reflection! How disgusting is that?

I needed to get out of that kitchen. But I also needed to find out what was going on. 'So what's all this about?' I demanded to know from Mum. That was when she told me. About Hugo. About Hugo being so clever that he had won a prize. I was just about to scream that life was so not fair when I caught sight of the letter Mum was waving. It was a letter addressed to Hugo. From the National Cold Centre.

disGUSTING litt creepy crawly

'Can I see that?' I asked in my sweetie-sweet voice, smiling in a way that Hugo would have been proud of.

'Such a clever boy,' Mum said, stroking Hugo's arm.

The letter said that Hugo had been invited to spend a week at the National Cold Centre – for half-term if he could make it. RESULT! The Flowerdews are such anoraks that they seemed to think that Hugo had won a prize. And Hugo is such

a plank that he couldn't remember that he hadn't entered a competition. But I don't care because Hugo is going to come back from half-term with a red nose — a bit like the cherry on Mum's cake!

   Dad started to pour his beer. Time for me to leave, I thought, so I left them to it while I went upstairs and started to think what kind of T-shirt I could make Hugo as his

*reward for catching a cold in the interests of modern
exploration! Sucker!*

 *TEXT from Xanthe: A! U GT 2 C THS RTCL IN
MAG! MEGA! X*

EYELASHES ARE SUCH
HARD WORK WHEN YOU
THINK ABOUT THEM

Xanthe and I read her magazine on the way to school. She told me about it on the phone when I rang her, but I still wanted to find out about it for myself. It was difficult because Tarqs was on the bus too, and I wanted to talk with him. In the end, though, I ended up saying Hi and then reading the article. After all, a boy couldn't compete with a magazine article. Not even Tarqs.

Because the article Xanthe had found in the magazine was all about models. It said that one of the top modelling agencies looked for models in one of the top London clothes shops. They hung out in the shop spotting the customers who

125

someone told him he looked like Brad Pitt— now he waves to all the girls we pass— SADDO

always eats 4 packets of crisps at break— every day!

still stin

he doesn't need to look quite so miserable, I'll talk to him in a minute

We're just SO excited about this magazine thing

were fab enough to be models. I finished reading it during a lesson, then I looked at Xanthe. She whispered, 'What do you think?' and I hissed, 'We've got to go!'

'That's what I thought,' Xanthe said. 'Next weekend?'

'You bet!' I replied.

And we spent the rest of the day talking about what we should wear.

Other than that it was a bit of a skanky week. So we spent a lot of our spare time working

We will definitely be the most talent talent anyone's EVER SPOTTED

biology— dead boring

on our outfits. Because Miss Pretty had made so many comments about our T-shirts we decided to work on some new ones. Those model hunters weren't going to miss us!

It was a good job that we did spend so much time at Xanthe's because whenever I did go home, my brothers were even more painful than usual. Ben was spending all his time rehearsing with GOB. So I never got to see Tarquin except when he was unloading the GOB gear into the cellar. I asked him if he wanted to come with me and Xanthe on Saturday. I told him why we were going, and he just gave me this look like he couldn't see why we'd want to do it. What is it with boys? They just don't get it!

looks like they're doing some sad routine

see? still the same old jersey

Heavy Metal lives

actually sounds quite good - spooky!

BOG OFF

NNE 1t

floor of Ben's basement

Hugo was a disaster area in the bighead department. He was so convinced that he was going to be a TV megastar because of his cold holiday, he rang up the local paper! How humiliating is that? I came home one day to discover he was being interviewed by some cheesy bloke who was taking his photo too! I AM SO NOT GOING TO TALK TO HIM IF HE ENDS UP ON THE LOCAL TELLY AS WELL!

oh, pass the sick bag per-lease

hope he hasn't used MY MASCARA on his eyebrows

PATHETIC

wonder if he's still got that squashed frog in his pocket

When he wasn't in the shop, Dad was also busy. He had been commissioned by someone to paint a huge picture of their grandchildren. It was to be in the style of a grand master. Per-lease! I ask you — how sad is that?

Fortunately, the week soon passed, and I managed to tell Mum where I was going with Xanthe on Saturday morning, just as she was taking one of her clients to sit with her upstairs. I don't think she could really have heard what I said, because she just said, 'Lovely, darling — see you later.'

Anyway, when Xanthe and I got to the shop, we made sure our make-up was OK before we went in. Xanthe looked extra fab, and she gave me a hug before we went in.

The article said that they looked for the models by the main doors, so we spent a lot of our time there. But we couldn't see anyone who looked like they were looking for models. Xanthe said that she thought it was because they kept themselves a secret. That meant that any of the people who were by the doors were potential model hunters. So we **decided** that we had to smile at everyone.

We got some dead funny looks. One woman came up **to** us and said, 'Are you looking at me? You got a problem or something?' She was freaky! I reckon she was the one with **the** problem! After that we moved away from the doors and pretended to be looking at the clothes. It was hard work grinning for so long. Xanthe suggested that we should try a more pouty look — like you see in the perfume ads in the magazines. That starts to hurt after half an hour too.

Sparkles

Totally Talented

glam

We found some more fringy stuff like I've got round my jeans

Are we gorgeous or WHAT?

I moved over to be with Xanthe as she looked at some jeans. How many pairs of jeans can you look at, though? We'd probably been in the shop for just over an hour when suddenly there was this tap on our shoulder. We thought it had finally happened! But then we turned round, and it was this security bloke leering at us. Surely he couldn't be from a model agency, I thought. Too right! He was so scary! He told us that if we didn't want to buy anything then we should go!

'Well!' I said in my most huffy voice. Then I gave him the evils, grabbed Xanthe and headed for the door. THIS DAY WAS TURNING INTO A DISASTER!

We were just about to go out of the shop when this woman walked up to us.

'Love the eyelashes! Are they real?' she asked, stroking Xanthe on the cheek. 'And where did you two get those fab T-shirts?'

Xanthe and I looked at each other. This woman was a bit Cruella de Vil and we weren't sure what to say to her. Eventually this strangled voice started to tell her that we had made the T-shirts ourselves. After a while, I realized that the voice was coming from me.

Then the woman gave us each a piece of card. 'Those lashes have potential, sweetheart,' the woman said. 'Call me. And I might be able to do something about the T-shirts too. Busy, busy!' she said, looking at her watch. 'Speaky soon!'

And then she went.

Xanthe and I just looked at her and then each other. Then we spotted the security man coming over to us again. So we left sharpish.

It was only when we were on the bus going home that we read the cards the woman had given us. It said she was from the Cat Walk Model Agency! I think it was a result, but Xanthe and I both weren't sure what result it really was.

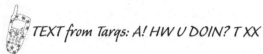 TEXT from Tarqs: A! HW U DOIN? T XX

WHAT IS IT WITH BOYS?

I was too busy talking to Xanthe to text Tarqs back. I mean, we were full of it on the bus home! The eyelashes, the T-shirts — the security guard! Some creep he was! I said to Xanthe, 'You are just so lucky to have those eyelashes — and they aren't even fake!' and Xanthe said, 'But you've got those great long legs!'

I have? I mean, I know I've got legs, but I didn't think they were particularly long ones. I tried to stretch them out under the seat on the bus, but there wasn't enough space. And anyway, the woman in the seat in front gave me a dead funny look because I think I'd managed to kick her.

Xanthe said, 'Do you think she was serious about the T-shirts?'

And I said I hoped so. But there was something creepy about that woman in the shop. Something a bit scary. I mentioned it to Xanthe, and she said she knew what I meant — she hadn't liked it when the woman had touched her cheek,

like Xanthe was a Dalmatian puppy she was going to make into a pair of gloves.

    Deee-sgusting!

    We sat for a bit in silence. If the woman hadn't said that we were the faces of the twenty-first century there'd kind of been no point in us going, had there? My phone beeped again. It was another message from Tarquin:

 *TEXT from Tarqs: R U CMN HM?*

    What was his problem? Course I was coming home — but what had it got to do with him? Xanthe made me feel bad because she said she thought that I was being mean to Tarquin by not answering him. She said he was my boyfriend after all.

136

Which was true. It's just a weird thing, this boyfriend stuff. You spend all that time wanting one and then when you've got one they kind of get in the way sometimes. So I sent Tarqs a text saying I was coming home, and I'd speak to him later. Then I asked Xanthe how her mum was.

She told me that she was thinking of changing her business! Instead of just importing and designing fabby jewellery, she was thinking she might do other things. But Xanthe said she didn't know what because her mum was still thinking about it.

Then Xanthe told me the mega news: that her mum and dad were definitely going to get divorced. Xanthe's eyes went all watery, and I just wanted to give her a big hug. But I didn't think I could do that on a bus, so I squeezed her hand instead.

I felt dead stupid because I couldn't think of anything to actually say to Xanthe that would make her feel any better. I mean pointing out that she would have two bedrooms instead of one seemed a bit pathetic when it was obvious that Xanthe would rather have one house with both her parents in it. Obviously my mum and dad are completely WEIRD but at least they are weird together – at the same time.

I was still holding Xanthe's hand when my phone beeped again!

 TEXT from Tarqs: R U THRE?

Tarquin was not going to give up, was he? So I sent a text back:

 TEXT to Tarqs: YS!

Seconds later he replied:

 TEXT from Tarqs: CMN 2 NONO? AM HR!

What was he doing at Nono's? Like was he spying on me? Xanthe giggled and said perhaps he was waiting for me because he wanted to see me – on account of being my boyfriend and stuff. I was embarrassed because I realized it might be true. I mean, Tarquin is my boyfriend. So we decided that we would go straight to Nono's to find out what was happening. Anyway, we knew that at least we'd get something good to scoff. And Nono would make us feel better after Dalmatian Woman.

The bus was getting closer to home when Xanthe said again that the woman had at least liked our T-shirts. We hadn't seen anything like them in the shop. Or on anyone else come to that. Ever.

'And making them is a good laugh,' said Xanthe.

True! I loved it when we started with a bog-standard, plain T-shirt and got out the sequins, beads and stuff. Then I had a mega-brill idea! I said to Xanthe, 'Why don't we make a T-shirt for Ms Pretty as a leaving present?'

Course Xanthe said that was a fabbo idea, and we spent the rest of the journey to Nono's talking about what it would look like.

Brian and Tarquin were winding some wool for Nono when we got there. That was when I realized why Tarquin was there. Because Nono was knitting the wool into a drum kit cover for GOB.

I love Nono so much. Every time I see Nono I remember all the reasons why I love her. And on top of that, she always smells of scrummy soap and fairy cakes.

Tarquin went all gooey when we walked in, and it was dead embarrassing because Nono patted to the seat next to her, and when I went to sit down she said, 'No, no, Xanthe can sit here. Why don't you go and sit next to dear Tarquin?'

BLUSH-OLA TIME! Per-lease!

EEEK! I'm on fire

hope my face doesn't clash with my T-shirt

Tarquin smiled and moved up his seat to make room for me. I sat down, but it was just so dead embarrassing! I needed to change the subject. So I said something about GOB and how good it was that someone was doing something to smarten up their act. After all, I said, they were just so drossy and were likely to look complete mingers on MUSIK MANIAKS.

Xanthe agreed, and we made Nono laugh when we told her about the positively disgusting clothes that they always wore. And we meant ALWAYS wore. Ben NEVER changes his clothes. I've never been down into the coal-hole, but I don't suppose he's got a wardrobe down there, full of other clothes to wear.

141

That was when Nono had her idea! She said why didn't me and Xanthe do something about what GOB looked like? She said we could design them some of our T-shirts to make them look more coordinated.

Tarquin looked at me and cooed, 'Will you make one for me too, Amaryllis?'

Talk about blush! He was so close to me when he said it I could feel his breath! In public! In front of Nono and

had to stop sitting next to Tarquin but even eating hasn't stopped me blushing

see, he can't take his eyes off me

it's so cool having a granny w can make good grub, li Nono

Possible outfit idea for Ben

big, brown sack with armholes

GOB

Xanthe! Who looked at each other and smiled! I think Brian was the only one who didn't notice. I mean, it wouldn't have been so bad if it wasn't in public!

Fortunately, Nono then said that she'd done enough knitting and who fancied a nice cup of hot chocolate with swirly piles of cream on top? Like we were going to say no?

And it was while Nono was in the kitchen making it that she said she thought she'd knit GOB some hats for the show.

 TEXT from phone company: U R OUT OF CRDT!

Oh poo!

EXIT SLIMY BROTHER STAGE LEFT

It was half-term. Normally I like half-term because:

☆ there's no school
☆ there's no homework
☆ I don't have to get up early in the mornings
☆ I can hang out with Xanthe
☆ I can go and see Nono during the day.

But this time, none of those things mattered. Because this half-term HUGO WAS GOING TO SPEND THE WHOLE WEEK AT THE NATIONAL COLD CENTRE CELEBRATING HIS PRIZE! Ha ha!

So this half-term I like half-term because:

☆ Hugo is going away for the whole week
☆ Hugo won't be here being all slimy
☆ Hugo won't be here being sucky uppy
☆ Hugo won't be in my way
☆ Hugo won't be playing with his worms in the garden
☆ HUGO WON'T BE HERE!!!!!

Hugo Poogo is so disgusting that he refused to let Mum pack his bag for him, and HE DID IT HIMSELF! Creep. Still, did he get loads of bags of sweets and Cheesy Wotsits to take with

him? He did not! Dad gave him some bags of wholegrain flapjacks to chew on instead. (These are completely disgusting things and impossible to chew on. It will take Hugo a week to suck halfway through just one and he has a Bumper Bag of twenty-four! Huh!)

Hugo was all smug and smiley and went off saying he was looking forward to the Chance to Help with Breaking New Scientific Frontiers. And spending all his time re-reading the Great Classic Books. Like yeah, right! Excuse me while I'm just a bit sick, Poogo.

Mum was weeping into a hanky as she waved farewell to Hugo when Dad took him off to the Cold Centre on the bike.

trembly earrings

trembly chin

Mum's farewell ode

snotty hanky

Just making sure that he really is going

trembly knees

I was having trouble trying to stop myself jumping up and down too much with J-O-Y!

YIPPEEEE!

Went straight round to Xanthe's to hang out with her. She told me BRILL news. That her mum has decided to open a shop! And it is going to be the shop next door to my Dad's (not so clever because this means that Dad will see me going in there every time).

Was just controlling myself after hearing this news when Xanthe said there was even better news on top! That Ms Pretty is going to be opening the shop with her mum! It is going to be a shop belonging to both of them. And it is going to be called Pretty Spicy!

Xanthe always has really interesting things to say

post-excitement hair

BABE

think I might make these shorter like Xanthe's

Even if I do not get to eat a single other chocolate crunchy cake at Nono's for the whole of half-term, this double-goody-two-shoes news, added to the fact that Hugo has GONE AWAY and will only return with a bunged-up nose, instantly makes this THE BEST HALF-TERM EVER in the History of Half-Terms.

Xanthe made us both some coffee, and then we went to her bedroom to drink it. I think that drinking coffee is dead cool: think Rachel in Friends and that woman in the adverts on telly. The problem is, though, that coffee is just disgusting to drink. It tastes yuck! What is the big deal about drinking coffee? And how am I going to start liking it so that I can look mega-cool?

Xanthe didn't seem to be drinking hers very much quicker than I was. I could tell she didn't like it much because she was kind of clenching her teeth with every mouthful she swallowed. So I said I was dead sorry but I thought the coffee was pants and could we have something different? Xanthe laughed and said she was glad I thought it was awful too, and we had hot orange squash instead.

We started talking about Pretty Spicy and how fab it was going to be. Tasmin had asked if Xanthe and I could think of the things we'd like to buy there so that she and Ms Pretty could work out what they should stock. Oh, like really hard work! We made a list and included:

☆ sparkly things
☆ shimmery things
☆ shoes with pointy toes
☆ things to put in your hair
☆ clothes with floaty bits
☆ stationery sets with matching staplers and paper clips
☆ make-up
☆ smelly stuff to put in the bath
☆ gorgeous things
☆ things my mum could buy me as presents that wouldn't make me want to die with embarrassment.

We finished our list and took it downstairs. Tasmin was busy at her workstation getting things organized for the shop. She said she loved our list and that she'd been thinking about the

T-shirts that we like to make. AND WOULD WE LIKE TO
MAKE SOME T-SHIRTS FOR THEM TO SELL IN PRETTY
SPICY?

Like she had to ask?!

We grabbed loads of craft stuff from Xanthe's bedroom and
shoved it all in a bag. We decided to go back to mine to work
on some T-shirts. After all, why make a mess in Xanthe's
gorgeous bedroom when we can make a mess in Hugo's
bedroom instead?

HUGO'S
BUGS
KEE[N]T

BODACIOUS
BABE

some sort
of slug
experiment

BAT
DETECTORS

WORM
FOOD

Xanthe's never
been this close to
a slug before

In fact, I had an INSPIRATIONAL idea when we got
to my house. After all, with Hugo Poogo away for a week with
his bogeys, we could not only use Hugo's revoltingly neat and
tidy bedroom to work in, we could also use his garden shed.
Result!

153

The only problem was, as we found out when we went in there, he still had lots of Revolting and DISGUSTING things in jars. A bit of a reminder of him, really.

 TEXT from Tarqs: CN I C U?

TEXT to Tarqs: MA B

T-SHIRTS AND TARQUIN

We spent the next couple of days making T-shirts, and it was great. Tasmin had given us a whole load of plain white T-shirts to work on. They were all different sizes. We made T-shirts for babies and even T-shirts for old people like my mum and Mrs Baxter.

We went round to Nono's to tell her about it, and she said we needed to give ourselves a T-shirt name so that everyone would know that the T-shirts were made by us. We talked about it over some cheesy scones, and in the end we decided that A 2 X was mega-cool. Nono said it was good, and she knew a place where she could get some proper labels for us to sew into the shirts to make them look professional!

Then she said did we want to use Brian as a model for one of the T-shirts. So we said yes and did a drawing of

155

Brian with a sparkly collar. We decided to make the collar textured when we got back to Hugo's bedroom.

Back at home, we could hear GOB doing their rehearsing while we worked upstairs. Even I had to admit that I was impressed by GOB working so hard for MUSIK MANIAKS. I even began to quite like their song. I'd heard 'I don't want to get out of bed' so many times, I almost knew it by heart.

Xanthe and I finished the GOB T-shirts but we decided that we wouldn't give them to the boys until the actual day of the competition. Which was on Saturday.

Tarquin was around the house a lot. He was busy doing all the roadie stuff. When GOB were taking breaks in between rehearsing, Tarquin kept on practising loading up the GOB van and making lists of the things that they needed to take with them to the telly studios. Boys are so sad, aren't they?

At first it was good having Tarquin hanging around. But he didn't seem to realize that Xanthe and me didn't really want him near us when we were busy with the T-shirts. And when you see someone every day of the week, what do you have left to say to them? OK, so I see Xanthe almost every day. But that's different. She's a girl. She's always got something to say back. Something interesting.

decided to
put Nono's knitted
fluffy stuff
round
the
bottom
↓

Frank △

NUTS

FRUIT

HOME
MADE
WINES

VEG

B

VIT
&
VIT

Supavi

NETT
BEE

HONE

HERBAL
TEAS

WINDFALLS

APPLES

Flo
SONS

Health Fo

One morning, Xanthe and I went to check out Pretty
Spicy to see how Tasmin and Ms Pretty were getting on. They
planned to open the shop fairly soon after the end of half-term.
Tasmin was going to run it on her own at first with Ms Pretty

working at the weekend. But as soon as school was over at the end of term, Ms Pretty would start to work there during the week as well.

The pair of them were clearing the shop up when we

159

arrived. They were getting rid of the stuff that had been left behind by the people who had had the shop before. Nearly fell over when we arrived because Tarquin was there! He said he'd agreed to help Tasmin and Ms Pretty move things about in the shop. It is beginning to get a bit creepy seeing Tarquin quite so much. That said, he is quite fit. So I suppose I can put up with it. And he is MY BOYFRIEND!

But DISASTER! We had only just arrived at the shop when my dad came in! He had seen us walk past and came rushing in with all these mugs of coffee. Well, actually, it was Dandelion Coffee. On account of the fact that my family is so not normal that they can't even drink ordinary coffee. Dad had made some coffee for me and Xanthe, which was a first. So it would have looked just a bit Not Cool to Not Drink it.

BIG MISTAKE! Ordinary coffee tastes pretty disgusting but Dandelion Coffee tastes FOUL! And I couldn't even spit it out! But fortunately my **dad** started to get all excited about one of the walls in the shop (yes, my dad IS that sad) so Xanthe and I gave Tarquin the mugs and asked him to chuck the coffee out in the street. Tarquin winked at me and said he would!

EEEK! hope Frank's really constipated to~

bet he hasn't washed the mugs

The Wall Thing was that my Dad reckoned that what Pretty Spicy needed was a mural on the wall. I was just beginning to hope that

a) he would shut up

or

b) the ground would swallow me up.

Pretty Spicy
high five
you are looking at the T-shirt queens
A 2X SWEET-SHIRTS R US!!

when I realized that not only Tasmin but also Ms Pretty thought that a mural on the back wall of the inside of the shop would look fab.

And Xanthe seemed to think that my dad's idea about making it an eastern theme to tie in with the Pretty Spicy thing was cool. And so did Tarquin.

Maybe my dad is just a tiny bit OK? Only maybe.

TEXT from Nono: CM 4 T?

TEXT to Nono: PLS!

IT'S THE GOB OFF!

The week whizzed by without Hugo getting in the way. On Friday, we all met up at school. This was not a mistake! The reason why we met at school was because it WAS half-term, and so school was empty, and Ms Pretty had arranged for GOB to be able to borrow the stage so that they could do a final rehearsal.

We all turned up. Even Melissa, Doug and Nappie. Nono was there, of course. She had made a mega picnic because, she said, we all needed Sustenance. Nono was wearing a GOB hat that she had knitted. I noticed that she had been as clever as usual and had made the hats that she and Mrs Baxter were wearing with special earmuffs. Presumably this meant that they didn't have to actually listen while they were pretending to!

Bearing in mind that GOB are GOB, and consist of my brother, Puke Face and Der-brain, GOB weren't too bad.

166

MY BOYFRIEND helping Nono check out one of her GOB hats →

remote control

GOB

← Brian modelling light-up GOB hat before the rehearsal

I mean, I knew that I wasn't going to positively die with embarrassment when I saw them on the stage at the telly studios. It was probably Tarquin's influence on them. But I still wasn't that sure that I wanted to look like a GOB groupie.

Big problem, though, would be getting out of wearing a GOB hat without being rude to Nono. I couldn't do that so Xanthe and I found ourselves wearing the same hat as my dad and Doug. SCARY MOMENT! Especially because Nono had put in some batteries so that the GOB bit lit up on our heads.

Anyway, GOB — get this — wore the A 2 X T-shirts for the rehearsal! Ooooo! Not bad. For GOB. In fact, excellent for GOB. When the rehearsal was over, Tarqs sat next to me and

Xanthe while we ate the picnic. He kept smiling at me and trying to hold my hand. Being a girlfriend is much harder than I thought it would be! I mean, how do you hold a boy's hand when you want to eat a chicken drumstick and swipe the last cheese straw before Doug does at the same time?

Also:

💡 What are you meant to say to boys?
💡 What are boys meant to say to girls?

169

💡 Are boys ever as much fun as girls to hang out with?
💡 Do all boys grow up to be like dads and Dougs?

If the answer is yes to the last question I will give up now ...

Saturday was the BIG DAY! GOB were getting themselves ready to go off to the telly studios and so Tarquin was mega-busy. Xanthe and I

helped him to get stuff into the back of
the van.

While we were doing this, Mum was in the kitchen
making GOB what she called a Good Breakfast to Get Them
Off to a Good Start. And Dad had gone off to collect Hugo from
the Cold Centre. Dad took ages to get back. But it was well
worth the wait.

Xanthe and I stood in the front room waiting for the
motorbike to pull up. And it was a Good Result when it did!
Because there was this little sidecar with its lid on. And all
the windows in the sidecar were steamed up. It was like a
little microclimate all of its own!

Dad parked the bike and got out before he opened the
door of the sidecar to let Hugo out. Hugo looked so awful I
almost felt sorry for him. He had

- a HUGE fat BRIGHT red nose
- watery eyes
- dry lips
- a spluttery cough . . .

and he looked even more disgusting than he usually does!

The bad news, though, was that Mum and Dad kept
pawing over Hugo because they wanted to know if he was all
right. They kept going all gooey over him and Mum even
called him her Little Hero! Per-lease! Hugo's nose was so
bunged up that he had to keep his mouth open all the time to
breath. And he had this really odd squeaky voice when he

171

I think he's got chilblains on his ears

really greasy hair

his specs are all steamed up!!

his nose looks like a rotten tomato!!

Giggles s if ing his snotty honkies - yuk

he, he, he!!

spoke. His pockets were full of snot rags too. Yuck!

Xanthe and I made sure that we kept well out of his way. This was for three reasons:

💀 Who wants to be near Hugo when he has got a stinky cold?

💀 Who wants to be near Hugo anyway?

💀 Who wants to listen to my mum and dad calling him things like Clever Boy and thinking he really has advanced Medical Research?

Fortunately, it was eventually time to see GOB off to the studios. We all lined up outside the house to wave them off.

Tarquin was the last one to squeeze into the van, and I helped to close the doors. I poked my head in to check that I wasn't going to squash him in the doors.

Tarquin quickly leaned forward as I did and gave me a kiss.

Bless!

TEXT from Tarqs: X

TEXT to Tarqs: THNX

GOB GROUPIES GET READY

As soon as GOB were gone, Xanthe and I went up to my
bedroom. This was not just to get away from Doug and Hugo.
We needed to have some serious getting-ready time.

Xanthe had found this magazine article that explained
How to Do the Perfect Make-Up. There was a list of make-up
that you needed, and between us we'd got most of it. What we
hadn't got we borrowed from Tasmin. After all, we could hardly
borrow any from my mum because the only make-up she wears
is disgusting pearly pink lipstick. How sad is that?

After doing face packs and stuff, it was about an hour
before we could start curling our eyelashes. Tasmin had lent
us this Mega Brill Eyelash curling machine. It made our eyes
look dead wide open and BIG. Then we put on

　☆ just a little bit of eyeshadow
　☆ some kohl

☆ some eyeliner

☆ some more eyeshadow

☆ some mascara — the stuff that makes your eyelashes go curly and long

☆ then we put on some blusher — just a tiny bit — before we put on some lipstick.

Finally we put on our GOB groupie outfits and Xanthe took my photo with her mobile phone (yes, she has just been given the latest mega teeny mobie by her dad) and then I took hers and we sent them to her dad for a laugh.

ready to rock →

sparkly scarves

Grunge Or Beauty

new mobie

We put glittery fluffy stuff round our jeans ↓

We painted glittery flowers on our shoes

When we were ready, we went downstairs. Everyone else was waiting for us in the kitchen. Getting to the studios was pretty complicated because there were so many of us. Nono had worked out the plan, which was dead cool:

☆ Xanthe was going to go in Ms Pretty's car with Tasmin.

☆ Melissa and Doug were going to go on their tandem and Nappie was going to be taken in the special baby carrier that they've made to go on the back (saddos).

☆ Mum and Dad were going to ride on the bike and Hugo was going to sit on his own in his Germ Pod.

☆ I was going to go in Nono's sports car with her, Mrs Baxter and Brian.

The only bad bit was that Xanthe and I couldn't travel together because Ms Pretty's car was small, and it would have

Nono always sings while she drives →

I LS th car ←

FABMOBILE

been a bit squished. Same with Nono's. The other thing was that I wasn't sure that dogs were allowed into telly studios, but Nono was so positive about it that I was sure that she would get Brian in, whatever the rules. And anyway, Brian did look cool in his GOB dog outfit.

Even in the GOB hat, it did feel quite cool turning up at the telly studios. There were all these people hanging around outside when we got there. Ms Pretty parked next to us so I was able to hang about with Xanthe straightaway. Xanthe said –

'Look, there's a telly camera over there!'

Which was true because they seemed to be filming all the families of the MUSIK MANIAKS performers going in to the studios. So Xanthe and I checked that we hadn't got lip gloss on our teeth and walked over to the camera in our best

think I might be a TV presenter, they get to wear gorgeous clothes

GOB

GOB

I'm pretty sure my hat is going to fall off

Xanthe is fluttering her fabby eyelashes

Gru Or B

Grunge or Beauty

I wave my arms around and knot my legs when I get overexcite

really high heels

Cat Walk walk. We made sure we flashed our T-shirts too.
And the presenter came and spoke to us! She asked us where
we'd bought our T-shirts. So we told her we'd made them,
and she said we were dead clever. And then she asked had we
made our hats for everyone as well, and we told her all about

180

Mega Nono. Then the presenter interviewed Nono and stroked Brian before cuddling Nappie. And that was it. We went in. I could get used to this celeb stuff!

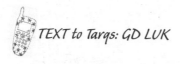
TEXT to Tarqs: GD LUK

No reply! Per-lease!

WITH T-SHIRTS LIKE THESE, WHO NEEDS BOYS?

It's actually quite sad how many people think they've got talent in this world. We had to sit through some real drongos in the MUSIK MANIAKS programme. In fact GOB were pretty good. But they didn't win. The winners were this girl band called the Shopaholics. They were pretty cool. A bit plastic but pretty cool.

GOB may not have won, but the brillo MEGA thing was that the presenter gave them a special mention. On account of their image! The judges said that they had:

☆ the best and strongest image of all the bands on the stage (but didn't have the talent to quite match it)
☆ great hats
☆ great T-shirts

☆ AND THE PRESENTER MENTIONED THAT
XANTHE AND ME HAD MADE THE T-SHIRTS AND NONO
HAD KNITTED THE HATS.

Result!

Ms Pretty said we were dead clever and told Mum and Dad that too! In fact, Ms Pretty even managed to persuade Mum and Dad to let me go home in the car with her and the others. Even though it was a squeeze for us all to fit in.

It was a real laugh being in the car with them. Tasmin kept saying how proud she was of us having done the T-shirts. And Ms Pretty kept on saying how pleased she was that they

would be stocking the T-shirts in Pretty Spicy. Then she said how great it was that the telly programme was going to mention the T-shirts too. Because she was going to make a big thing about the opening of the shop and invite the local paper along to it!

Just then my phone beeped.

 TEXT from Targs: U R COOL!

Like he thought I didn't already know?

It was pretty boring to have to go back to school on Monday. Except that news got round pretty quickly about GOB. They

boiled school
cardigan for
the bolero effect

school tie can be
trendy if carefully
tied

always stick sequins
on buttons

beaded T-shirt
by A2X!!

Self portrait
bag - very
Now

carefully laddered
tights to give that
groovy ribbed look

painted shoes

the only way to wear school
uniform

may not have won, but everyone seemed to think it was a
result that they had come second. Xanthe and I couldn't wait
for them all to actually see the programme – especially when
they went on about the GOB outfits!

Xanthe and me went round to Pretty Spicy every day
after school with Ms Pretty. We were helping get the displays
sorted. And Dad was there finishing off the mural. He seemed
to have left Ben and Frank in charge of the shop. Which meant

that he must have been dead keen to do the mural to leave two such useless items to run the shop.

The mural was taking ages, though! And you could tell that Tasmin and Ms Pretty were getting a bit anxious about

when it was actually going to be finished. After all, the Grand Opening was quite soon. And they couldn't finish everything else in the shop until the painting was finished.

So I asked Dad when he thought it would be finished, and he explained that some of the filling-in bits were taking him a long time. Then he asked if we could help him. Cool! Just a shame that Tarquin kept hanging around and telling me how clever I was. What is he after?

Seemed like mega ages before it was the Grand Opening but it finally happened. And it was brill. Pretty Spicy looked gorgeous. It was sparkly and full of

things that I wanted to buy to wear or have in my room. Even better, Tasmin and Ms Pretty owned it and they had said we could have a discount on some of the stuff! And our T-shirts were on sale.

The nerdy man from the local paper was there. He spoke to Ms Pretty and Tasmin and then took their photos. My dad made sure he stood in the background with a cheesy grin. My mum was there, wobbling her earrings, and she kept on saying, 'Really, you girls, I had no idea that you enjoyed sewing.'

Does my mother know anything about me? Not!

But then this glitzy woman came in to the shop and walked over to Tasmin and started talking to her. The woman was wearing these mega-pointy-toed shoes, and she looked so cool with a slinky skirt on that flicked out at the bottom. Xanthe and I were like — wow! And we just stared at the woman as she chatted with Tasmin, who was pointing things out to her around the shop. We were still gawping at her when we realized that Tasmin was pointing at us!

Then they came over to us! The woman was called Scarlet, and she said that she was the reporter from GLAM

wish my hair was all curly like this

Mum said this bag would cost LOADS — but Mum's probably got it wrong

makes a swishy noise when she walks

ooooh!

Miss Glam Times

TIMES magazine, and she was going to do a feature about
Pretty Spicy, and would we let her take our photograph? Like
she needed to ask?

After that, Ms Pretty did a speech telling everyone
about the shop, and everyone clapped, and it was cool. Then,
dead embarrassing, Ms Pretty said OUT LOUD, would Xanthe
and me be prepared to do some modelling of some of our
T-shirts because everyone had said how original they were.

Dead embarrassing but dead brill. We did our
slinkiest walks across the shop and back. It was mega. Then
Nono joined in with Brian. Which was cool. But it was not
cool when Mum decided that she could wobble some earrings
for everyone. Has she got no idea? Obviously NOT!

these are
the bangles
Xanthe gave
me

NONO
ROCKS

Sugar
Plum

100%
perfect

I just know we'll be snapped up by Models One at any moment

Eventually everyone started to go home and the Grand Opening was over. I was going to go home with Mum and Dad when Tarquin stopped us and said he could walk me home. Mum and Dad gave us these soppy grins and winked at each other before they went. Per-lease!

But I didn't want to go off with Tarquin! I wanted to think about T-shirts and the next lot that Xanthe and I could make. Tarquin just wouldn't get it if I talked about them with him.

Tarquin tried to link his arm in mine as we walked along the road. I told him someone might see! But then he tried to do me a full-frontal snog! What is he like? I pushed him away, and then he kind of sulked the rest of the way home. Boys!

At the gate,
Tarquin said that now
GOB were resting after
MUSIK MANIAKS,
could he hang out with
me after school every day? I
told him that I hung out with
Xanthe — didn't he know
that? And he said that he
thought that now that he
and I were an Item
that would change!
What is he on?
Item? What does

he think I am? They have signs in supermarkets saying 'Four items or fewer', don't they? Does he think I am a box of cornflakes or some frozen peas?

So I told Tarquin that I did not have time to hang around with him every day because Xanthe and I had just gone into business together making T-shirts. If he liked I could see him on Thursdays and every other Saturday. And if he didn't like it that was just too bad.

Then I went into the house and shut the door. I peeked at Tarquin through the spy hole in the front door. He looked a bit sad standing there on his own. Well, that's his problem.

eyehole spyhole

Just how long is he going to stand on the doorstep?

That night, I lay in bed thinking. Not about Tarquin but about A 2 X. I reckoned that if Scarlet and GLAM TIMES were so interested in our T-shirts then it was a dead cert that OK! and HELLO! would soon be in negotiation for pics of Xanthe and me 'At Home Making Their Sensational Trendy T-shirts'. We could spend the money from selling the pics on buying our own flat!

Seems like Xanthe and me have managed to get from A 2 X quite nicely, thanks!

ALSO BY
CAROLINE PLAISTED
& CHERRY WHYTOCK

What do you do when you were born to be a star but your family's the most embarrassing on earth? Imagine if your dad painted pictures of nude women who looked like your mum and your younger brother liked homework (and experimenting with your bra in the garden).

Amaryllis has to cope with that – and more. Find out how she does it in her hilarious journal, fabulously illustrated by the girl herself.

GWYNETH REES

Daniel knows that his mum was very ill once – mentally ill. She's fine now, and she's even landed a big new job as a head teacher. The problem is, she's head of his new school. It's so embarrassing!

Just as Daniel is trying to fit in and make new friends, his mum stops taking the medicine that keeps her well. As she starts behaving more and more weirdly, Daniel realizes that something is terribly wrong. His mum is ill – and he is the only person who can help her . . .

A selected list of titles available from Macmillan Children's Books

The prices shown below are correct at the time of going to press.
However, Macmillan Publishers reserves the right to show new retail
prices on covers which may differ from those previously advertised.

All Pan Macmillan titles can be ordered from our website,
www.panmacmillan.com, or from your local bookshop
and are also available by post from:

Bookpost, PO Box 29, Douglas, Isle of Man IM99 1BQ
Credit cards accepted. For details:
Telephone:+44(0)1624 677237
Fax: +44(0)1624 670923
Email: bookshop@enterprise.net
www.bookpost.co.uk

Free postage and packing in the UK